ALPHA ACADEMY
THE FINAL TEST

NAMES: *Skye Hamilton, Charlie Deery, Allie A. Abbott*

AGES:
Wise beyond our years.

HOME:
Is where the heart is — Alpha Island.

HOW YOU WON DARWIN BRAZILLE'S HEART:
I never lost it in the first place ;)

BEST ALPHA ACCOMPLISHMENT:
Believing that I truly belong.

BIGGEST CHALLENGE AHEAD:
Proving it to Shira.

TOP OF THE FEUD CHAIN

A
TOP OF THE FEUD CHAIN

AN ALPHAS NOVEL BY
LISI HARRISON

poppy

LITTLE, BROWN AND COMPANY
New York   Boston

Poppy
Little, Brown and Company
Hachette Book Group
237 Park Avenue, New York, NY 10017

For more of your favorite series, go to www.pickapoppy.com

First Edition: May 2011

Poppy is an imprint of Little, Brown and Company
The Poppy name and logo are trademarks of Hachette Book Group, Inc.

The characters and events in this book are fictitious. Any similarity to real
persons, living or dead, is coincidental and not intended by the author.

Cover photo by Roger Moenks
Author photo by Gillian Crane

alloyentertainment
Produced by Alloy Entertainment
151 West 26th Street, New York, NY 10001

ISBN: 978-0-316-03582-8

10 9 8 7 6 5 4 3 2 1
CWO
Printed in the United States of America

Clique novels by Lisi Harrison:

THE CLIQUE

BEST FRIENDS FOR NEVER

REVENGE OF THE WANNABES

INVASION OF THE BOY SNATCHERS

THE PRETTY COMMITTEE STRIKES BACK

DIAL L FOR LOSER

IT'S NOT EASY BEING MEAN

SEALED WITH A DISS

BRATFEST AT TIFFANY'S

THE CLIQUE SUMMER COLLECTION

P.S. I LOATHE YOU

BOYS R US

CHARMED AND DANGEROUS

THESE BOOTS ARE MADE FOR STALKING

MY LITTLE PHONY

A TALE OF TWO PRETTIES

Alphas novels by Lisi Harrison:

ALPHAS

MOVERS & FAKERS

BELLE OF THE BRAWL

TOP OF THE FEUD CHAIN

For Amelia Kahaney and Lucy Keating. Every Alpha letter on every Alpha page of this final Alpha novel is evidence of your talent, dedication, and hard work. Thank you, my lollies.

ALPHA ISLAND
LAKE ALPHA BEACH
NOVEMBER 1ST
11:27 A.M.

"Kick her butt, Skye!" Charlie Deery's forehead throbbed with tension as she squinted out at the race on the sun-flecked lake, but she forced her hands to keep clapping in support of her bestie. Riding the choppy waves in the final stretch of Alpha Academy's stand-up paddleboard regatta, Skye looked like the goddess Aphrodite emerging from a clamshell—only instead of a clamshell, she stood atop a paddleboard, and instead of flowing silks, Skye wore pewter boyshorts, a silver rashguard, and a look of ferocious determination in her aquamarine eyes.

Charlie curled her bare toes in the lake's phosphorescent green sand and anxiously nibbled her cuticles. Skye was one of only two paddlers left on the racetrack, which was marked by buoys shooting glowing holographic lines that hovered a foot above Lake Alpha. If she won, the Jackie O's would stay on Alpha Island for at least one more day. If she lost . . . Charlie shook her head, sending a few strands of her long mahogany hair blowing in the manufactured gale-force wind, and tried not to focus on the waterlogged losers dragging themselves to shore.

If Skye lost, her suitcase would be waiting. And her time as an Alpha would be up faster than the Situation's shirt.

Sailing by the recently capsized board of Shoshana Shanti-Smith from the J. K. Rowling house, Skye's toned back flexed into an aggressive stance. Her dancer's poise had made overtaking the other six paddleboarders look easy, but now she had to pick up enough speed to kick the flat booty of spoken-word champ (and surprisingly gifted paddler) Spinnah Fraye from the Queen Elizabeth house. The kinky-haired Spinnah was six foot two and built of pure muscle, but now that the race was nearly over, she seemed be losing steam. Her paddling had turned sloppy and her muscular legs wobbled atop her board. In comparison, Skye looked more alive than ever, pushing her oar through the turbulent water as if stirring a giant Frappuccino. Still, Spinnah held her lead on Skye to at least three board-lengths.

Charlie shivered and felt her platinum bomber vest grow sleeves as it registered her chill. As long as Skye remained in second place, not even body heat–activated clothing could warm the icy panic she felt inside.

Take her out! Charlie whisper-yelled, putting a tense hand in her pocket and crossing her fingers, telling herself to have faith in her dancer roommate. If anyone could beat Spinnah, it was Skye. The Jackie O's were lucky to have her representing them in the Paddle Battle—both Charlie and fellow O Allie A. would have sunk faster than soggy cereal in milk, but Skye skimmed the water like a hot pool boy.

Aside from today's nerve-wracking board brawl, Charlie had a lot of reasons to feel lucky. In fact, for the first time since enrolling at in Alpha Academy— the mega-exclusive school created by Shira Brazille, TV personality, CEO, and Alpha-in-chief—Charlie had everything she wanted. After weeks of bouncing between Darwin and Allie A., her one true love and first true best friend, everyone was finally happy. Thanks to Charlie's brilliant matchmaking, Allie was attached at the metallic-mini hip to Melbourne, Shira's ice-blond eldest son. Which meant that Charlie could finally go public about her rekindled relationship with Darwin, the only boy she'd ever cared about. The boy she'd known since she was five years old and her mother, Bee, began as Shira's assistant. At last, there were no more secret rendezvous behind Allie's back, no more necessary visits to the Zen Center every day just to calm her nerves. Now that Allie and Charlie were both happily hooked up, their days on the island had taken the agony out of agonizing and left the zing.

Especially lately, now that Shira had stopped hovering over the island like an après–bean burrito smell. The bossy Aussie had been away on an unexplained business trip for nearly two weeks, and aside from these crazy competitions, Charlie's life was finally simple.

Maybe this time it would stay that way.

Charlie sucked in a mouthful of crisp lakeside air and turned her coffee-brown eyes to the row of volcanoes that ringed the lake in the center of the @-shaped island. Sighing, she considered the years of planning and technological wizardry needed to build this tropical biosphere in the middle of the Mojave Desert. Not to mention its surfable faux-cean. Originally, one hundred girls had been chosen from around the world to attend Alpha Academy, but soon it became clear that they weren't so much here to learn as to compete. One by one, or sometimes in mass-firings, Shira gave Alphas the axe. The fall semester wasn't even over and already one hundred girls had been whittled down to thirty.

As Bee's daughter, Charlie had participated in the building of this (wo)man-made paradise. She had watched Shira scour the world for the most brilliant dancers, actresses, designers, mathematicians, scientists, hackers, and writers for her Academy, and they had all eagerly signed up to study at the most exclusive school ever created. Their teachers were world-class, their classrooms state-of-the-art. And yet here they were, paddling hard but going nowhere.

Charlie watched a pair of soaking-wet Alphas drag themselves to the sandy shore, hair matted down on their defeated faces.

Charlie's worry-wince flattened into a pained smile as she thought back to the Alphas' response when Shira first announced her emergency business trip. Everyone had gone nuts over the thought of being unsupervised, and the island instantly ignited with late-night bonfires, impromptu fashion shows with nonregulation outfits, and a rewired sound system perfect for blasting the new Kanye album.

But the party didn't last for long. Soon, being the competitive Alphas they were, the girls began to invent competitions. And that was when it became clear what Shira's plan was from the start. Before she left, Shira had prophesized, "One girl will make herself known. One girl will stand above the rest as a leader." Like an estrogen-fueled remake of *Lord of the Flies*, the girls quickly abandoned their parties and set about vying for control. And the house muses—the camp counselor–types who mentored each Alpha house—responded in kind. For every contest, they awarded a prize. The bunk that won the goat-milking contest on the island's organic farm got to control the weather on the island for twenty-four hours. The house that bested the rest at the *Alice in Wonderland* all-night giant chess match got makeovers and leadership coaching.

And the losers were sent home.

Last night, she and Allie had made a list on her aPod of who had been kicked out and why. After the Paddle Battle was over, there would be at least seven more additions. Charlie opened up her Alpha Tracking App and reviewed the latest executions.

ALPHA CUT	DIDN'T KICK BUTT
Hillary Clinton House. Dakota LeMercier, chemical engineer/aromatherapist.	Lost an impromptu pie-eating contest—allergic to blueberries.
Joan of Ark House. Yuki Asukawa, shoe designer/geologist.	Lowest scorer in Big Top Relay Race. Her attempt at fire-juggling got her (and her hair) fired.
Beyoncé House. Anastasia Vallessi, opera singer/quantum physicist.	Fell off her board during a sky-surfing competition and landed in a baobab tree.
J. K. Rowling House. Willow Dawn, landscape architect/urban farmer.	Tripped her polo pony with a mallet misfire.
Mother Teresa House. Martha Mulvaney, actress/screenwriter.	Choked during a spelling bee. Literally. And was unable to perform her own Heimlich. Couldn't spell it, either.

Tyra House. Chavez Moreno, activist/political cartoonist.	Dismal performance at Alphas karaoke contest. Instead of "Hit Me Baby One More Time," she sang "Hit Me Maybe One More Time."

There was only one person who could have sent them packing. Charlie squinted up again at the distant volcanoes, wondering where Shira had hidden her surveillance cameras on the picturesque lake. Probably inside the buoys, she decided. Shira was definitely watching their every move. Because only one girl would be left standing at the end of the semester. Whoever it was would be the ultimate Alpha, or—how had she put it? Charlie searched her memory for the icy Aussie's exact words. An *Alpha for life*. No one knew exactly what that meant. They just knew they wanted it.

With Alphas challenging each other every day, even the sweetest of the remaining Alphas had embraced a kill-or-be-killed mentality. Everyone felt the pressure—no matter how ah-mazing their accomplishments, their time here was running out faster than single Jonas Brothers.

Charlie sighed and scanned the beach, wishing Darwin were here for moral support. Among the noncompeting spectators were three of Spinnah's housemates, including video-game designer and makeup junkie Louise Holtstropper.

"Let's go, Spinnah, make Skye a swimmah!" she cheered. Charlie rolled her eyes at the pathetic rhyme—Louise should leave the spoken-word to her bestie. Snapping her attention back to the Paddle Battle, Charlie's breath caught in her throat. Skye and Spinnah were rounding a hairpin bend in the course, and Skye was now just inches away from Spinnah's board! *Go go go*, she whisper-chanted, her heart pounding with renewed hope.

Just as Skye's board drew up next to Spinnah's, one of the rhyme-azon's spoken-word poems floated across the lake to reach Charlie's ears.

Check the sunset, forget the horizon
Skye's gonna meet the water like Motorola met Verizon!

Then Spinnah punctuated her poem in the form of an oar aimed at Skye's shoulder.

No! Charlie gasped along with the crowd, everyone's eyes glued to the last two fighters in the regatta. The wind seemed to pick up in pace with their rapidly beating pulses. Charlie's stomach capsized, but Skye's board didn't. She righted herself as only an exceptional dancer could. Instead of falling sideways from the force of the blow, she reached out a flailing hand and grabbed Spinnah's oar, yanking it from her opponent's grasp and righting herself in the process.

"Wooo!" The crowd went crazy, rippling with a mix of envy and pride at Skye's risky move. Spinnah wobbled on her board but remained upright. Only now she had to paddle out of her way to retrieve her oar. *Come on, Skye. This is your moment.* Charlie closed her eyes and sent up a prayer to the water gods to let her friend survive. When she opened them again she noticed Louise hopping up and down with excitement, then stopping to check her hair placement in a compact mirror.

A moment later, the two floating fighters disappeared into the final leg of the course, a holographic wave-tunnel that looked like a solid wall of churning water. Whoever emerged first would immediately cross the neon-pink finish line hovering in front of the tunnel. Charlie swallowed a lump bigger than Snooki's hair pouf and waited for the victor to emerge.

Charlie turned back to the lake just in time to see the nose of a paddleboard emerging from the holo-tunnel.

Please let it be Skye!

And then she spotted a foot. Followed by a slender, ballet-toned calf. An overjoyed Skye sailed out of the holo-tunnel, her platinum wavelets shimmering, her fingers like two V's held high in victory.

"YES!!!" Charlie screamed, tossing her aPod in the sand and running into the heated lake toward her beaming friend. The Jackie O's would live to see another day on

Alpha Island! And maybe, just maybe, they would find a way to make it to Shira's ultimate finish line together. But then what? Charlie pulled Skye into a celebratory hug and tried her Alpha best not to think about it.

2

THE PAVILION
ELIXIR SMOOTHIE BAR
NOVEMBER 1ST
12:42 P.M.

Skye Hamilton step-ball-changed her way along the glowing green counter of the Academy's smoothie bar, Elixir. Located in a freestanding glass cupola just off of the dining hall and surrounded by the lushness of the rainforest, Elixir felt like an oasis within an oasis. Skye pressed the touch screen embedded in the countertop with wiggling jazz fingers. "One strawberry-banana-guarana-bee-pollen-protein-powder-blast yogurt coming up," the Yo-Bot behind the counter announced, a neon-pink line of LED lights forming a pulsating robo-smile.

"Thanks," Skye told the bot, pirouetting around as Charlie placed her order. Skye was positively giddy after her win, her brain now flooded with the kind of butt-kicking endorphins she hadn't felt in ages. The constant threat of being sent packing tore her confidence like a tutu in a tug-of-war. She couldn't imagine how Beta the losers must have felt rolling their suitcases down the dock while their friends fake-pouted with better-you-than-me-pity. Lately, wheel sounds of any kind brought on a flash flood of pit-sweat—a condition now known among the Jackie O's as Roll-o-phobia. But she was safe for now.

Sigh-smiling as she wound her platinum-blond wavelets into a bagel-sized bun, Skye closed her eyes and let her mind drift back to the Paddle Battle. Once it was just Spinnah and Skye in the holographic tunnel, Skye was still behind enough to do something drastic. The tunnel was her last chance. Just then, the water gods sneezed a gale-force wind their way, quickly turning the tunnel into a vacuum tube. Skye ripped her headscarf out of her hair, fashioning a sail by tying it to her paddle and lifting it to catch the breeze. She sat down on her board, using her dancer's posture to let the wind do the work. Spinnah paddled harder and harder, but even her long, ultra-toned arms were no match for Skye's sail. In a moment of panic, Spinnah shoved her paddle into the water at a desperate angle and lodged it into a sand bar lurking just below the surface, catapulting her over her board. Skye sailed through the opening of the tunnel with a huge smile plastered across her face, and she didn't look back.

"Tell me again what Spinnah said when her paddle got stuck in the sandbar," asked Charlie, reaching across the counter to grab their smoothies.

"Stuck in the sand, man, I need a third hand," giggled Skye as she plunged a recycled aluminum straw into her cup's lid. "Not one of her best."

"You were the only one of us who could have won that competition," Charlie mused, taking a thoughtful sip of her mango-wheatgrass brain booster. She tipped her head back to catch a bit of sunshine coming through the glass ceiling of the cupola. "I would've been the first girl to capsize."

Skye shrugged, her lips pursing as she took a long, indulgent chug of her smoothie. But Charlie was right. Stand-up paddle was a lot like dancing on water: The timing had to be perfect, the moves steady. Triple Threat, her former roomie and fellow dancer, had taught her to anticipate the water's rocking motion and to use it to her body's advantage . . . before she had tried to get Skye kicked out of school.

Elixir's doors swooshed open, letting in the algae-tinged smell of lake water combined with the talcum tickle of pressed powder. The fragrance was soon followed by Louise Holstropper and the rest of Spinnah's housemates, each of whom looked Skye over with a toxic mix of anger and envy.

"Hey, Skye. Great job out there," sneered Louise. Louise was from Texas, and as far as Skye knew she only cared about two things: makeup and video games. (She'd already invented and sold two of them to Sony—ProStylist and ProStylist Oscar Edition, where the player had to get celebs

ready for the red carpet during a catastrophic earthquake.)
Short in stature with a button nose and a limp brown bob,
Louise used more base than Bob Marley. And wore so much
blush everyone had thought her forehead was bleeding the
first time they saw her perspire. "Wild guess as to who taught
you that last move," Louise added, wiggling her penciled
brows knowingly.

As the QE's encircled her, Skye felt her cheeks grow hot.
She knew Louise was referring to Taz, Shira's most extro-
verted son. Taz and Skye had spent many a windy day on his
boat, which he moored on Lake Alpha. They had tried to
keep their romance under wraps, but just like Justin Bieber
and Selena Gomez on their Caribbean vacation, word got
around.

"I don't know how Shira would feel about you getting an
unfair advantage from a boyfriend, let alone her own son,"
Louise smirked, her over-lined lips reminding Skye of the
Joker from *The Dark Knight*. "Good thing you don't have
that problem anymore."

The beautiful glass room now felt like a glass cage as
Skye's sea glass–colored eyes searched her surroundings for
some moral support, but Charlie was oblivious, busy repair-
ing a stuck gear on the Yo-Bot. Louise's words stung, but not
because of Skye's competitive side. For the past few weeks,
she had been trying extra hard to scrub thoughts of Taz from
her mind, focusing on her Alpha objectives instead. But Taz

wasn't easy to forget. His playful ice-blue eyes, inky black hair, and life-of-every-party confidence met all her crush criteria. Taz was like a Sharpie—impossible to erase no matter how hard she tried.

Skye thought back to their last interaction. It was on the Muse Cruise, where even from the center of the dance floor, surrounded by a circle of blinged-out Alphas bending backward under a limbo stick for his attention, his eyes had locked with hers and sent more heat through her muscles than an entire tube of Bengay. Obviously there was still something between them. Or so she wanted to believe. But every time she'd seen him since, he'd brushed her aside like he was Jake Gyllenhaal and she was Taylor Swift. Clearly, Taz had no intention of forgiving her for the biggest mistake she'd made at Alpha Academy—briefly dating his emo brother Sydney. No matter how many times she hoped and dreamed he would.

Skye rolled her toned shoulders back and elevated her B-cups, jutting her chin out in a stance of rock-hard confidence she hoped looked believable. "I can take you anytime, anywhere," Skye muttered to Louise, lifting a recently pruned eyebrow. With thoughts of Taz revving her heart, Skye's competitive fighter spirit kicked in hard.

Louise inched close enough for Skye to notice a gray glob of eyeliner lodged just below her lash line. "Then how about a PAP race?" she dared her. "We all know you have balancing skills. Let's see how you do in the sky, Skye."

Skye's breath caught in her throat. She had zero pilot experience in the Personal Alpha Planes. Meanwhile, Louise was an engineer who specialized in video game design. Her technical ability would surely put her Kabuki'd face in the lead. Skye struggled desperately to find a way to bow out of the over-glammed gamer's challenge. A fear of heights? Small (spherical) spaces? A sprained groin muscle from ferocious paddling? But at this point refusing to compete was another way of saying, "Why, yes, I'd love to pack up my wheelie suitcase and roll it across the dock while you snicker. Sounds great!"

Still, there had to be another challenge. Just as Skye was about to suggest a parasail dance contest, her aPod pinged with a new message. She pulled it out from the pocket of her hoodie, trying to buy a few extra seconds and hoping it wasn't a text from her dance teacher, Mimi, telling her to get her ballet buns to class.

Charlie: I pretty much invented the software for PAPs. I've been flying since I was 12. With me as your copilot, we can't lose.

Yay! Skye's spirits soared. Her genius inventor friend had been paying attention after all, and she was ready to take on lame Louise in a PAP battle. Skye looked back at Charlie, now perched cross-legged on the smoothie counter and whistling casually to herself. They exchanged a quick wink.

Turning back to Louise, Skye grinned confidently. "Pick your copilot and meet us at the runway tomorrow at high noon." She wasn't totally sure what "high noon" meant but knew it sounded more intimidating than "twelve" or "lunchtime."

Louise raised one highlighted brow, a smug half-smile emerging on her powdered face. "Can't wait." Skye was annoyed by how confident Louise seemed. In fact, all of her housemates, with their bad hair and bad posture, seemed a little too confident.

"You lose, you leave," Skye added, just to make sure Louise knew she wasn't scared, even though she was.

"Same goes, big toes," Louise smirked. The other girls chuckled.

Skye executed a full pirouette. *Big toes my foot!*

"Looking forward to watching you sashay yourself off this island." Louise pulled out a giant compact and searched her round mirror for pores that had long been buried alive. Then the wannabe geisha spun around on her gladiator sandals toward the glass doors, which immediately opened to reveal—Mayday McGrath, the best stunt flyer on the island.

Uh-oh.

17

Skye gulp-gawked, noting that Mayday was already dressed in a platinum flight suit and aviator glasses, her Raggedy Ann–red hair tucked into a flight helmet and a cocky smile playing on her lips. She told everyone her parents were Blue Angels who had fallen in love in the air. As soon as she was tall enough, Mayday spent summers doing air stunts and winters driving in NASCAR races.

Ugh! Skye's eyes searched for Charlie's, but she just shrug-smiled, as if to say *no biggie*. Skye could have sworn Mayday had been expelled weeks ago, after a go-kart race she organized down Mount Olympus went awry and two girls ended up with concussions. Skye stared up at Mayday's long, narrow face and attempted a smile, but her mouth refused to cooperate.

"You look pale," Mayday remarked, her aviator glasses slipping toward the end of her nose until she pushed them back up. "Don't tell me you're worried about a little PAP race."

Mayday was like a bald eagle—awkward and twitchy on land, fearless and beautiful in the air.

"Of course not," Skye bluffed.

"Great. May the best flier win," Louise said smugly, sauntering over to Mayday and putting an arm around her copilot. "After we beat you, we're going to write QE'S 4-EVER in the air."

Skye didn't need a pilot's headset to hear the QE's message loud and clear: With Mayday aboard, winning this race would be cake. And Skye and Charlie would wind up creamed.

3

JACKIE O HOUSE
LEISURE GARDEN
NOVEMBER 1ST
3:13 P.M.

In the dappled shade of a jacaranda tree, Allie A. Abbott settled back into a white leather chaise lounge next to an excited Charlie and Skye, feeling more relaxed than she had in days. After Skye's victory in the paddleboard regatta that day, Allie, Charlie, and Skye had decamped to the private garden behind Jackie O to regroup, relive the win, and strategize their next moves, protected from prying eyes by a wall of vines and passionflowers. Every so often, an inspirational quote projected via hologram slid across the sky above them. Currently the phrase *Regret for Wasted Time is More Wasted Time* was gliding out of sight. Allie shut her eyes and took a whiff of the hydroponic African violets, planted in a scripted A formation on the garden's lawn beside them.

"I mean, Louise actually thought she could intimidate Skye of all people," Charlie's voice was an octave higher than her usual measured tone as she sat perched at the edge of her chaise, facing her two lounging companions. "Just wait. We will *so* take her down in the PAP race, Mayday McGrath or no Mayday McGrath. We're on a roll! And then she'll be right back in Tucson."

"Fresno," corrected Skye.

"Same thing," said Charlie, who'd lived all over the world.

"Mmm," Allie murmured, stretching and wiggling her manicured fingers. "I wish I'd seen it. I was with Mel—"

Charlie cut her off, still too jazzed to keep from planning their win. "We'll take Darwin's PAP. He's got it all tricked out . . ."

Allie was only half listening to the words coming out of Charlie's mouth. She sighed contentedly, relieved to finally be a part of the team. After faking her way into Alpha Academy by impersonating Allie J. Abbott, the reclusive folk-rock sensation whose acceptance letter got sent to her by mistake, then being exposed when the real AJ had showed up, the drama was finally behind her. Except in the classroom, of course. Forcing herself to carry on while everyone ostracized her for lying had brought out a passion for acting in Allie. And now, she not only had a direction in life, but she'd managed to get her friends back and rebuild her reputation. She could finally walk the manicured grounds of Alpha Academy without dirty looks pelting her like rubber bullets. No more Alphas sneaking whole milk into her skim latte. No more hate-texts sent from anonymous addresses. And best of all, no more mistrust between Allie, Charlie, and Skye.

With Alphas dropping faster than pounds on *The Biggest Loser*, people had better things to do than rehash old betrayals.

At least, most people did.

Allie shot her navy blue eyes over to the floor-to-ceiling windows of the Jackie O House and grimaced as she caught sight of AJ alone in the Jackie O study lounge. The petite folk singer was belting one of her new songs into a microphone, enormous headphones covering her multi-pierced ears, her grubby green tam slouched on her head, wiggling her tiny butt as a 3-D holographic crowd projected onto the wall cheered her on.

Ugh! Couldn't she go five minutes without attention?

Allie shook her head slightly, her thick honey-blond hair tickling her back. She was just about to turn away from Jackie O and focus again on Charlie and Skye, but then AJ whirled around to face the garden, her moss-green eyes making contact with Allie's navy ones like hate-seeking missiles. AJ lifted one of her tiny, hemp-buttered hands, and Allie braced herself for a taunting, finger-wiggling little wave. Instead, AJ ran her index finger across her neck in a slitting motion, her Burt's Bees–waxed lips mouthing the words "You're compost."

Clearly, the green queen hadn't gotten over Allie's little stunt at the Muse Cruise two weeks ago. With AJ stuck at home with the flu, Allie had decided to impersonate her one last time. She'd set up a brilliant Ashley Simpson–esque lip synch scenario for the partygoers, and it had worked . . . a little too well. Everyone truly believed that AJ was a fraud. Now AJ was hell-bent on revenge.

Allie ignored the ice-cold feeling in her veins and concentrated again on Charlie, who was now busily drawing flight maneuver formations in the dirt with a stick.

"And when Mayday really starts showing off," Charlie said, waving her stick in a crazy-8 pattern in front of her, "that's when we throttle ahead—"

Skye shifted uncomfortably in her chaise longue, lowering her voice just in case Louise or one of her minions was listening in. "I know you love a challenge, Charlie, but winning this race is major. It's life or death. Alpha Island or Staten Island. And let's be honest, Mayday is an ah-mazing flier. There's a very real chance we might go home tomorrow."

Allie sat up, her spine stiffening when she heard the word *home*. "Won't happen," she said, much too quickly. "It can't."

But Skye was right—it was possible. But after everything she'd been through to earn her besties back, Allie wasn't about to lose them over some Queen Elizabeth–inspired air show.

Her stomach gurgled, and it wasn't just late-afternoon munchies. It was the sick realization that unless she found a way to guarantee victory, her two best friends would be kicked out by this time tomorrow and she'd be stuck with AJ all alone in Jackie O. She nibbled at an errant cuticle on her thumb while scouring her brain for ideas. Sugar in the QE's gas tank? No, the planes ran on biodiesel and electric. Ex-Lax in Louise's morning tea? If only she had some. Maybe Mel could send one of his brothers to bat his boy-lashes at Mayday so she'd miss the race altogether? And then it came to her. *Taz!*

"You guys must have forgotten that we know the best fliers on the island." Allie jumped out of her chaise while simultaneously pulling her aPod out of her pocket.

"Uh, no kidding, Allie. Mayday is the best," Skye said glumly.

"Better than Mayday," Allie said patiently, waiting for Skye and Charlie to get it. But they just stared at her, their eyes emptier than a brand new hard drive. "The Brazille boys started flying long before even Charlie did. I have an old *Us Weekly* somewhere that says Taz successfully landed a small aircraft at nine years old. " Allie turned to Charlie. "True or tabloid?"

"True," Charlie nodded. "They were all flying before they were ten, but Taz is definitely the most fearless."

"Do you really think it's a good idea?" Skye interrupted,

her voice crackling with nerves. "I mean, everyone's watching. How will we even get them onto the plane without Louise noticing?" Skye turned to gaze at the blue-green faux-cean visible in the distance through a gap in the garden wall.

Allie's eyes met Charlie's, silently communicating her agreement about needing to get the boys' help. Skye was obviously just anxious about being near Taz. Every time his name had come up lately, she got all quiet and un-Skye-like.

When they'd first started at the Academy, Skye and Taz had seemed destined to be the Brangelina of the island. But then Skye had started dating Syd, Taz's brooding older brother. Skye's feelings for sulky Syd had soured faster than milk in the tropics, but Skye had to fake being into him under strict orders from Shira, who thought she was finally curing him of his emo ways. And even though Skye and Syd had long since broken up, Taz had never gotten over it. He wanted nothing to do with her, even though it was clear as the water in Lake Alpha that Skye still adored him.

"Skye," Allie said quietly, putting a hand on her friend's toned, sinewy shoulder. "I'm not letting you give up. We have to start taking risks. Shira expects us to, and I think she'd actually approve of our ingenuity. With so few girls left now, only the sneaky will survive. Trust me, I know," she giggled softly.

Skye sighed. "I guess."

Allie walked back over to the chaise longue and perched on the edge of it, trying to think of a plan to get the Brazille boys onto the plane. They hadn't been a part of any Alpha-on-Alpha competition, because as Shira's sons there was no way they'd be kicked out. They'd never be Alphas for life, but they'd never be sent packing, either.

"Well, Allie?" Charlie plopped down next to her. "You'd better be formulating a brilliant plan and not just daydreaming about Mel's pretty eyes," she warned before joke-nudging her friend in the arm.

"Thinking . . . shhh . . ." Allie muttered. Mel did have pretty eyes, she smiled to herself. *Wait, that's it!* "Ohmuhgud, Charlie. You are a genius."

"What'd I do?"

"We have to make them pretty. Pretty enough to pass for girls!"

As Skye and Charlie giggled and began discussing what color eye shadow would work best on each Brazille boy, Allie took out her aPod and started to type.

Allie: You know how you always say you'll try anything once? How about a little makeup and an Alpha uniform? We need you to fly in a PAP race with us tomorrow.

She hit send and waited, hammering her index finger against the side of the phone impatiently.

Ping!

Mel: Always knew my legs would look good in a mini. But Taz and Darwin are way better. Not the legs, the flying. My legs are def the best.
Allie: Can you get them to help?
Mel: I'm the oldest. They have to do what I say.
Allie: Thx. Makeovers 4 downunders. Can't wait!

Allie slid her aPod shut. "Mel's in, and he'll convince Taz and Darwin. But he seems more into the idea of wearing my clothes than the actual flying. Should I be worried?"

Charlie bit her bottom lip. "Only if he can't zip them up."

THE BRAZILLE RESIDENCE
THE GREAT ROOM
NOVEMBER 2ND
11:10 A.M.

Skye lay curled up in the corner of a giant white leather L-shaped couch in the Brazille mansion's great room, trying to take up the least amount of space possible and stay out of harm's way. *And out of Taz's way*, she thought glumly, ducking her head to avoid being hit by a mascara wand as Charlie tossed it to Allie. Skye had expected Operation Beautify the Brazille Boys (OBBB) to be hard, for Taz to glare at her and take some cheap shots. But it was worse when he was pretended she didn't even exist. Kind of awkward when they were stuck in a room with only four other people. Luckily for Skye, Syd's heart had recently been crushed by yet another Alpha, Seraphina Hernandez-Rosenblatt, and to cheer him up, his brother Dingo signed them both up for a celebrity motorcycle race across Africa. They'd left a few days ago, and with any luck they would continue racing around Africa for the foreseeable future.

Skye shudder-gagged at the thought of the unfortunate African girl who would have to deal with Syd's smothering affection next. She'd take being ignored by Taz any day over that.

Still, Skye couldn't help sneaking peeks in Taz's direction. Allie stood over him, struggling to pull the coppery wig she swiped from the props room over his thick brown hair. "Stay still," she grumbled. Skye could see stress-sweat accumulating on her friend's forehead. Getting the Brazille boys to look like girls had been a bigger project than any of them would have guessed.

"Do I seriously have to shave my legs?" Darwin yelled from the landing, worry creasing his tanned forehead. He aimed his hazel eyes at Charlie and ran a nervous hand through his wavy light brown hair.

"Yes!" Allie, Skye, and Charlie all yelled back in the same exasperated tone.

"Seriously?" Darwin tried again, the cinnamon-flavored toothpick he chewed on wobbling as he spoke. "I'm a manly man. It's gonna take forever."

"That's how long it will be before you see me again if we get sent home," Charlie said, sternly placing her hands on her hips. Darwin sighed and then stalked toward the bathroom.

"Some girls don't shave their legs," said Mel, struggling to pull a pair of silver leggings up over his own lower half.

Allie whipped her head around to glare at her boyfriend. "Alphas shave."

"Except AJ," Charlie reminded her. "She claims she's naturally hairless."

Skye envied Charlie and Allie for the easy banter they had with their boyfriends. Back in Westchester, Skye had always had her pick of guys to choose from. And even here, she'd had no problem finding two Brazille brothers who were interested. For the millionth time, she wondered what on earth had made her choose Syd over Taz, then inwardly kicked herself for not being able to prove to Taz that she'd picked wrong.

A minute later, Darwin clomped back downstairs in a pair of low-heeled booties, wearing a silver Alphas bubble skirt, a white blouse, and a thin silver cap-sleeved cardi, his legs now girly-smooth and smelling like baby oil–scented shaving cream.

"What would Mom say if she saw us now?" Darwin ran a hand through his honey-brown locks, looking terrified.

"Let's just be glad she *can't* see us," Mel chuckled. Skye gave her housemates a wary look. *If only they knew . . .*

"Dude, you're a pretty cute girl." Taz joked, springing out of his chair wearing nearly the same outfit as his brother. "Metallic really makes your eyes sparkle." He almost toppled over, then glared down at his metallic wedge heels.

"You too," Darwin snickered, knocking Taz in the ribs.

"I had no idea you had such toned calves. You must have logged some time at the dance studio when you and Skye were dating."

Skye froze. She looked up at Taz, whose ice-blue eyes caught hers for an awkward second before looking away. Luckily, their discomfort-bubble was popped by Mel.

"Do my legs look bulky? Be honest." The eldest and tallest Brazille brother, clad in silver leggings and a boatneck blouse, did a slow turn for Allie, sending Skye and Taz into simultaneous fits of hysterical laughter.

Regaining composure, Skye wiped her eyes and blinked at Taz. She wondered if maybe they stood a chance after all. Wasn't a similar sense of humor the foundation for any relationship? Maybe this little PAP excursion wasn't all bad. At the very least, it could be her chance to finally explain to Taz why she'd chosen Syd.

Fifteen minutes later, Charlie, Allie, and Skye emerged from the residence dressed in platinum flight suits, clear gladiator sandals strapped to their feet and aviator glasses on their heads. They walked side by side with the three Brazille brothers—manicured, wigged, and done up in full Alpha-glam style.

"Remember your posture," Allie reminded the boys. "Shoulders back, chest out, hips swaying. The wrong kind of gait could be a dead giveaway." Mel, Taz, and Darwin nodded like hungry pupils.

"Man, being a chick is rough," Skye heard Taz mutter under his breath.

Trying to appear as natural as possible, the six of them began to make their way across the island. As they walked past the great lawn, Skye nearly crashed into Taz, who had stopped to eavesdrop on two bikini-clad Hillary Clintons and a Beyoncé sunbathing on giant gold towels.

"Oof! Keep walking!" Skye whisper-shouted. "You're wearing a dress, remember? It's going to seem a little funny if you keep checking out other girls."

"Hang on," Taz murmured, his ear cocked. Skye crossed her arms and strained to hear what could be so fascinating.

A Snooki-colored Hillary Clinton took a swig from an aluminum water bottle. "No contest. Taz is totally the hottest one. He's Efron and Lautner put together."

"And he's the best dancer," added Blair B., smoothing a layer of sunscreen over her shoulders. Blair was a championship figure skater and budding film director from the Beyoncé house. Not only was she like Skye on ice, she'd already screened three movies at Sundance. Even under his girly makeup, Taz's face glowed with pride. He gave himself a self-congratulatory nod.

Skye's blush was deep and immediate, like an allergic reaction to shellfish. Her stomach lurched, and she swallowed hard before her morning muesli made a reappearance in her mouth. Taz was cocky enough, and Skye certainly didn't want to hear how coveted her crush still was now that they weren't together. She put her hands on Taz's back and shoved, hard. He staggered back on his platforms and shot her an annoyed look.

"What?" he said. "I heard my name!"

"How do you know they weren't talking about another Taz?" Skye shot back, exasperation mixed with flirtation warming her like an après-dance hoodie. "You think you're the only guy on the planet with that name?"

Charlie and Allie stifled their giggles, or at least tried.

"Uh, yeah." he smirked. Skye wasn't sure, but she thought she detected a molecule of playfulness in his voice. She stared at his broad-shouldered back as they walked single file toward the hangar and tried to take her own advice: *Eyes on the prize.* Was it her or were they getting more glances than normal? Alphas were notorious for their once-overs, but this felt different. Skye picked up her pace. The faster they got to the hangar, the sooner this whole thing would be over.

"Wow," Skye whispered, her aquamarine eyes widening as she stepped across the threshold of the decahedron-shaped PAP hangar. It smelled like fuel, fresh paint, and the year 3000.

Light streamed in from all ten sides of the enormous structure, illuminating row upon row of specially designed gold aircraft. Skye had never bothered to visit the hangar before, but she vowed that if she ever had the chance to sneak back at night, she'd throw an ah-mazing party here.

"Charlie, tell me you've flown one of these things," she called out, pointing to a plane that looked like a shiny black boomerang and another smaller aircraft that seemed composed entirely of chubby silver tubes with a tiny seat in the center.

Charlie whirled around on her feet and flashed Skye a lopsided grin. "I wish. I mostly stick to PAPs and the occasional jet-pack."

"Yeah, me too." Skye giggled. "Not."

The group came to the PAP launchpad in the middle of the hangar, where two perfectly round bubble-shaped planes awaited them. Charlie had already been there early this morning to choose their vehicle—Darwin's PAP—and she hopped inside to check that all systems were fully operational while Allie and Skye waited casually on the platform for Louise and Mayday. Meanwhile, the three Alpha "girls" hustled into the backseat of the plane, whisper-laughing as they smacked each other's skirted butts.

"How will we all fit?" Skye whispered to Allie, who was busy using her aPod to check the coordinates of Louise and her QE flight crew.

"Shhh, they just walked in the north entrance of the hangar."

Skye hurriedly began stuffing her copious white-blond waves into a cute flight helmet she'd swiped from one of the Frisbee-planes, straightening up just as Louise and Mayday strutted onto the platform. Mayday's headgear was just like Snoopy's—an old-fashioned leather number from the 1920s. Her neon-red hair peeked out below it, and her green eyes twinkled with calm amusement as she sized up Skye and Allie.

"She almost looks like a real pilot," she quipped to Louise, whose carrot cake–colored face wrinkled in a fit of laughter.

"That almost looks like a real tan," Allie shot back.

"Let's go over the route and start flying," Charlie called from inside the plane. "So we all agree we'll fly forty miles east across the Alpha ocean toward Mojave and through the desert until we go above Flowering Cactus Mountain. Then we'll circle back," Charlie said, her hands busy checking the readings on the PAP's touch screen.

"Yep." Lou nodded up at her, her brick-red lips forming a confident half moon. "First PAP back wins."

Charlie stuck her head out of the porthole of their plane. "I'm bringing some friends for moral support. 'Kay?"

"Fine with us," shrugged Mayday, zipping up her metallic bronze flight suit. "Bring as many people as you want— they'll just weigh your craft down."

"They don't weigh as much as Louise's makeup bag, so we should be okay," Skye snapped.

Before Lou or Mayday could come up with a response, Skye half-pirouetted around on her heel and skipped toward the plane.

"All right." Taz pulled his fake hair back into a ponytail with surprising skill and adjusted his aviators. "Everyone buckled in?"

"Yes," the group responded from their squashed seats.

"Everyone ready?" he asked. The reply this time was more hesitant, but Taz didn't seem to notice. "Great. Let's do this." And with that, he pulled back the controls and the PAP soared swiftly into the air.

High above the island, in a PAP packed tighter than Kim Kardashian's Spanx, Skye studied Taz's profile in the cockpit. He was copiloting next to Charlie, but they took turns maneuvering the round little aircraft along the unpredictable air currents of Shira's woman-made biosphere. They hadn't been flying long, but what little air there was left in the PAP was already filled with tension. Charlie was right, Taz was a good pilot. But Mayday McGrath was excellent.

"Left, left!" Darwin yelled from the backseat. Skye covered her left ear, which was uncomfortably close to Darwin's head. "You need to get more torque going before you flood the gas." Everyone who wasn't actually flying the plane—Darwin, Skye, Allie, and Mel—sat squished together behind the cockpit in a second row of flip-up flight seats.

Allie turned. "I thought these were electric planes."

"The computer system runs on electricity, but the planes run on biodiesel unless they're coasting," Charlie said from the front.

Skye turned to gaze behind Darwin's big head out the window at the competition's aircraft, whizzing back and forth just behind them. Through the translucent glass of Louise and Mayday's PAP, Skye could see two sets of hands gesturing wildly and two flame-red mouths moving quickly, talking over one another. Even with only half the people in their PAP, they looked as miserable and stressed-out as the Jackie O's. Apparently, things weren't going as well for them as Louise had predicted. They'd been neck and neck for the majority of the race, but for now the Jackie O's had a slight lead.

The sound of Allie's perfect ski slope–shaped nose sniffing the air brought Skye's attention back to her own team. "Does anyone smell that?" Allie asked.

"What?" Charlie asked nervously.

"It's . . . kind of like McDonald's French fries," Allie said in a confused tone. She licked her glossy lips. "Yum."

"Forget the food court, Allie, they're pulling ahead," Charlie replied. "Gun it, Taz!"

But Skye smelled it, too. She looked at Allie and raised her eyebrows.

"Darwin, did you leave an old Happy Meal box in here?" Allie asked.

"Yeah, 'cuz my mom is always taking us to the drive-thru," he joked.

"Seriously," giggled Mel, adjusting part of his leggings. "It reeks like McFarts."

Everyone burst out laughing. And then the engines went from roaring, to sputtering, to completely silent. The plane was just . . . floating; a runaway balloon drifting in the afternoon breeze.

Skye could hear her own heartbeat thudding in her ears.

Calmly, Darwin said, "Everyone buckle your seat belt. Now."

Everyone started to scream.

5

They were plummeting. Charlie tried everything. She gunned the gas. She flipped on the autopilot. She pushed the manual override icon so hard her thumb turned purple. Nothing. The plane was responding slower than a deadbeat boyfriend. Behind her, half the gang was screaming and the other half sat eerily silent, stunned by fear, as the gold edges of the PAP plane shuddered around them, jolting from side to side.

"Taz," she screamed. "What are we not thinking of?"

But Taz just let out a choked groan, his hands alternately clutching at his wig and then typing commands into his touch screen. "Everyone, brace for landing."

Ohmuhgod. No no no no no.

"Do something!"

"Are you serious?"

The screams and cries from the backseat floated up to

Charlie's ears again, but she couldn't absorb them. All she could hear was her own internal scream. She felt a hand on her shoulder and turned to find Darwin, unable to remove his seat belt, straining toward her desperately. She knew he was trying to communicate to her that everything would be okay. But would it?

In the seconds between the air and the earth, time slowed down. The best moments of Charlie's life played before her like a 3-D movie trailer. Her mother, Bee, holding a three-year-old Charlie on a Brazille-chartered cruise ship from mainland Africa to Madagascar. Six-year-old Charlie swimming through cliffside caves in Fiji with Dingo and Darwin. Her first slice of New York pizza, at age eight, also with Darwin. Hot springs in Iceland. Snowshoeing outside of Anchorage. Everywhere, every memory, every image had Darwin flitting somewhere in the frame. Then Alpha Academy. Dancing at a beach bonfire with Allie and Skye, tinkering blissfully for hours on her latest project in the Academy's light bulb–shaped inventor's lab. The face of her mentor, Dr. Irina Gorbachevski, floating toward her with a helpful critique of Charlie's latest invention. And then there was Darwin's face again, swimming toward her, his arms embracing her . . .

Ka-thunk!

They were down.

She was alive.

Charlie stopped screaming and opened her eyes to peek out the windshield, but just then the plane began to ricochet back into the air.

Ka-thunk!

Down again.

Of course! Remembering the patented bounce technology she had helped to create, Charlie gritted her teeth as the plane bounced to a stop along the hard-packed earth of the Mojave Desert, her body slicked with sweat under her flight suit and her nerves more frayed than Miley Cyrus's cutoffs. Rebound technology meant the plane was retrofitted with rubberized shocks, but never in a million years did Charlie think she'd experience the "pogo effect" she'd helped invent in anything other than a simulated crash.

Charlie's tear-filled eyes searched the control panel in front of her, but all indicators were still dead. The control panel's screen matched the landscape—blank, desolate, barren. In large contrast to the PAP, which was a mess. Wigs were scattered everywhere, blankets and oxygen masks had fallen from overhead compartments. It was total chaos.

Taz whispered from the copilot's seat. "I don't crash planes. I crash parties. I thought these things had manual backup systems."

"So did I," she whispered back.

Charlie just couldn't understand it. This model was the

result of fifteen years of research by Brazille Industries—it was the most technologically sophisticated aircraft on Earth! And if Charlie remembered correctly, the PAP had three backup systems in case of engine trouble. How could all three have gone bust at once? She smacked the flat of her palm onto the screen, a move she hated seeing other people try when they had a tech glitch. But even though she knew it wouldn't work, she kept on hitting, unable to stop.

Finally, Darwin placed his hand on hers, his fingers circling her wrist. "Stop, Charlie. We're okay. We landed. Don't go beating a dead PAP."

Charlie nodded a silent *thanks*, put her now-throbbing hand in her lap, and looked over at Taz. Seeing that he was shaken but unharmed, she twisted around to check on everyone in the backseat of the plane.

"Is everyone okay?" Charlie whisper-cried. Darwin's hand had found her shoulder during the crash and squeezed, and now that she could see him, the tightly-coiled panic in her chest began to unspool a little.

Darwin smiled at her, his hazel eyes filled with relief. "All good back here. You're not hurt, are you?"

Charlie wiggled her fingers and toes and did a few neck-rolls just to make sure that, unlike the PAP, all parts of her were in good working order. "I'm okay," she sighed. "Physically okay. Mentally, the jury's still out."

She turned to scan the freaked-out faces of Mel, Allie, and Skye. The backseat contingent had gone from screaming to silent, as if a mute button had been activated during the crash. Skye was pale. Allie's gaze floated forlornly past the PAP window while Mel wrapped his arms tighter around her and whispered something in her ear. They all appeared stunned and scared but physically unharmed.

"Um, guys?" Skye said, breaking the silence in the PAP. She tapped a polished fingernail on the window. "Where are we? Everything is so . . . beige."

Allie pressed her nose against the window. "I think we landed in a Pottery Barn catalogue."

Had they not just crashed in the Mojave Desert, Charlie might have laughed. Miles of cracked earth, cacti, tumbleweeds, and a few mountains with smooth plateaued tops in the distance were all she could see. Water, food, shade, and shelter, not so much. Nightfall would be their downfall if they didn't get out of there soon.

"I'm sure Louise and Mayday will come for us," Allie tried.

"Don't be," Skye huffed. "I saw them waving goodbye as we began to fall."

Don't start panicking, Charlie, she told herself sternly. Reflexively, she reached for the three cameo bracelets she always wore on her right wrist. Inside each cameo was a picture: one of Darwin; one of her mom, Bee; and one of her

DD (dead dad—he'd died in a plane crash before she was born, and touching his picture sent a shiver down Charlie's spine. They finally had something in common).

Channeling Alpha Academy's resident yogini, Samsara, Charlie rested her hands on her knees and attempted some meditative breathing in a desperate attempt to achieve calm.

Slow, deep breath in, deep breath out.

Repeat.

But all breathing did was help Charlie focus on just how serious their situation was. And the more she thought about it, the louder her heart thumped out its panicked SOS.

Resolving to solve the problem methodically, Charlie pulled out her aPod. Step one was obviously to figure out exactly what their coordinates were so she could call in a backup unit. But when she tried to get a signal, her aPod screen flashed:

SIGNAL NOT AVAILABLE BEYOND ALPHA BIOSPHERE.

No problem, Charlie swallow-nodded. Every PAP came equipped with a GPS locator.

She pressed a small silver button etched into the smooth white ceiling above her head, sending an ovular, pill-shaped

GPS device about the size of a soda can into her lap. But when Charlie powered it on, all that came out was static. Frantically, she began turning a dial on the side of the GPS, waiting for a signal.

"*No signal?*" Charlie heard Allie cry out behind her, and realized her bestie had been able to see the screen. "Does that mean we're never getting out of here?"

The rest of the group erupted into high-pitched jabbering and arguing about what to do.

"*Guys.* Calm down," Charlie said as calmly as she could. "Of course we are. There should be a way to override this . . ."

But every channel was the same: a cold, lonely buzz, like the howling of a black hole in deep space. A sound that signaled not just the end of their lives as Alphas, but the end of their lives, period.

Charlie's hands fell to her sides and her heart followed suit, sinking in her chest. "This isn't good," she moaned, putting her head on the white A-shaped steering wheel in front of her.

The inventor in her was still diagnosing the PAP's engine failure, but the Alpha competitor in her was devastated, certain that now that they'd lost the race, she might never get the chance. And if all systems were truly dead, it wouldn't be long until they would be, too.

Keep calm and carry on, Charlie thought-chanted to herself. Her mom had always used this expression when things seemed dire.

"It's all Skye's fault!" wailed Allie.

Fear is contagious, Charlie remembered. If she acted afraid, everyone would follow suit. Her flight crew would soon turn on each other, which wouldn't help them figure out a way out any sooner.

"No, Allie, it's nobody's—" Charlie tried to cut in before tensions rose, but Skye yelled over her.

"My fault?" Skye shrieked. "I wasn't flying the plane. I was just sitting here trying not to watch you make out with your boyfriend when we started sinking—"

"You're the one who agreed to this PAP race in the first place," Allie hissed. "We're lucky to be alive right now."

"Okay, yeah, but was I the one who had this brilliant idea to sneak the boys onto the plane?" Skye yelled. "If I remember correctly, that was one hundred percent you, Al. And we probably went down because the plane was too heavy. Right Charlie?"

Mel whipped off his wig. "Stop attacking Allie!" He put a protective arm around her shoulders. "If my brother was as good a flier as he claimed—"

"Oh, shut up, pretty boy," Taz snort-replied. "If it were up to you, we'd still be doing each other's nails right now."

It was so loud inside the PAP that Charlie couldn't hear herself think. Only Darwin managed not to join in the shouting match—he shook his head in bewildered disappointment.

"SHUT! UP! EVERYONE!" Charlie yelled, projecting her voice louder than the entire cast of *Glee* put together.

Yelling wasn't Charlie's style. In fact, she never did it. It was so unlike her that it actually worked. Everyone looked at her expectantly, so she lowered her volume and continued. "We all played a part in this. We didn't think it through carefully, because we were so eager to win. We were careless. We made our beds, and now we have to lie in them."

"You mean die in them," Allie said sourly.

Charlie's shoulders slumped. The last thing she felt like doing was giving the group a pep talk. She needed to think. That was how she worked in the inventor's lab. A bunch of fighting, squawking voices would only make her mess things up even further.

She reached behind her seat and found Darwin's hand. She gave it a desperate squeeze, hoping to communicate all this to her intuitive-beyond-his-years boyfriend.

Darwin must have understood her unspoken SOS, because he piped up immediately, using his calm surfer Zen-ergy to cheer everyone up. "We're hungry, tired, and we don't know how or when we're getting out of here. But the good news is that Charlie practically invented the PAP technology. She'll figure out how to get a signal again, and hopefully have the PAP running in no time. The other good news is that there's a ton of bottled water behind my seat, and at least twenty BrazilleBlast bars."

"Thank God," Allie sniffed, still obviously upset at Skye but willing to move on. "I'm starving."

Darwin distributed the snacks, and everyone reluctantly stepped out of the PAP into the blindingly bright sunshine of the Mojave. Charlie stayed aboard solo, determined to get the GPS up and running as quickly as possible. While she worked, she heard Mel, Darwin, and Allie rigging up a shade structure by tying a tarp to the plane's tailfin.

Time ticked by, and Charlie continued to work, doggedly trying everything she could think of. Finally, the door of the plane opened and her sandy-haired boyfriend stuck his head into the cockpit.

"Here. You need to drink," Darwin smiled and passed her an A-shaped aluminum canteen with a glittery pink shoulder strap. "How's it going?"

Charlie smiled up at him, wishing she had better news to report. She took a cautious swig from the aluminum canteen, knowing they needed to conserve water. "Thanks." She tried to smile, but the corners of her mouth were like the PAP—down and out.

"We'll get a signal soon." Darwin's face remained calm and reassuring. Charlie should have felt better, but she still wasn't convinced. Darwin was a great musician, an awesome cook, and a skilled surfer, but he wasn't a techie. All he had was blind faith that Charlie could fix anything. And right now, she wasn't sure that was true.

6

In the deepening dusk of the Mojave, the horizon was edged with a blue-gray haze that seemed to stretch on forever. Skye's Tiffany box–blue eyes flitted over the landscape searching for signs of life—headlights from a car or plane, flashlights from a search party, camera lights from a news crew—but the only visible movements were the aimless tumbleweeds rolling across the desert floor, like abandoned beach balls after a pool party.

Behind her was the downed PAP. Charlie sat hunched in a circle of shade beneath the snub nose of the useless aircraft, clutching the silver GPS unit in both hands like it was a Magic 8 Ball about to deliver a fortune. It delivered static. Some future.

Just past some boulders to Skye's left, Darwin, Mel, and Allie squatted around a circle of rocks they'd filled with thin gray sticks, dried-out cactus husks, and long yellow seed pods they'd collected from the desert floor. They'd managed to singe a few leaves using sunlight refracted through Allie's sunglasses, but so far the fire was anything but raging. It belched an occasional puff of smoke, and they'd need a lot more than that to stay warm in the rapidly darkening night.

Without the blazing heat from the sun, the desert was getting colder by the minute. Sighing, Skye wrapped her leg warmer–covered arms across her midsection and tried to keep herself calm. Just as her internal panic reading was veering from orange to red, the quiet desert was blanketed by the thudding bass of a Jay-Z song.

Huh?

She whirled around to try to see where the sound was coming from, and spotted Taz sticking his head out of the window of the cockpit with a huge grin plastered on his face, head-bobbing along to Jay-Z's "Empire State of Mind."

Skye couldn't help dancing a little, too, matching Taz's gorgeous smile with a grin of her own. At least if they were going to die out here, they could have a little fun before being forced to drink their own pee or fending off a pack of rabid coyotes. When Taz turned and flashed his grin at her, she felt more alive than ever.

"This is no time for a dance party, bro," Darwin yelled over the music, stalking toward the plane with an armful of tumbleweeds and an annoyed expression. It looked like he'd just cleaned out the drain in the Jackie O shower.

"It's the perfect time!" Taz yelled from the back. "This is the first time since school started that we're under zero supervision. No cameras, no muses, no schedule, no rules. We should be making the most of it." His pale blue eyes found Skye's blue-green ones and quickly flicked away, but not before a warm, gooey excitement spread through Skye's chest like Nutella on a fresh crepe.

Taz was right—they should enjoy this experience as much as possible. Not that she could resist his charm either way. Skye let her hips shake slightly to the beat while her feet moved her toward the PAP, pulled as if by an invisible magnet toward the source of the sound. She sang along to the lyrics:

These streets will make you feel brand new

Just then, her stomach growled like Mike Tyson's tiger in *The Hangover*.

The lights—gurgle—*will inspire you.*

Skye put a hand on her midsection, trying to keep it quiet. She wanted hot food, not another BrazilleBlast bar. She had the metabolism of a leopard, and sugary bars weren't cutting it. Too bad the bars were all they had . . . or were they?

Skye froze mid-booty-shake, thinking back to when the plane was going down. She must have blocked it out during the panic, but in all the jostling and bumping she distinctly remembered seeing a large satchel fall out of the back wall, a reflective wrapper peeking out from the top.

Before Skye second-guessed herself, she took a running leap up the stairs extending from the PAP and plopped down next to Taz in the cockpit. He looked up from a play-list he was making and raised his thick eyebrows, shooting her a quizzical, wary glance.

Wariness was better than outright hostility. Skye would have to take it. She smiled, took a breath for courage, then grabbed Taz's arm and pulled him behind her to the back of the plane. "Come on. I think I know a way to make this party even better."

"Why do I have to come?" Taz protested, but Skye didn't answer, hoping that if her memory wasn't playing tricks on her, he'd like what he saw.

Skye crawled awkwardly over the backseat of the plane and smiled when she spotted the canvas bag where it had fallen out of the rear of the PAP like a dead body. She dove for it, and sure enough, under the canvas were several cans marked Pork 'N' Beans and Corned Beef Hash, along with two bags of powdered mashed potatoes and a dozen packets of hot chocolate—enough food for a huge dinner tonight! Skye's salivary glands were instantly activated, and her smile grew even wider she spotted the matches, flares, blankets, and a few more A-shaped canteens.

"Nice!" Taz yelled, giving Skye a high five. His light blue eyes glowed with genuine appreciation as he flashed her one of his lopsided, girl-magnet smiles, indicating that the wall of ice between them was definitely thawing. "This is awesome!"

And for the first time in a while, Skye truly felt awesome. Not only was she going to make sure everyone was toasty and well-fed tonight, but her relationship with Taz might be shifting from life support back to alive and kicking.

Back outside, Darwin leaned against a boulder as he used an aPod app to strum virtual guitar strings along to the music. Mel and Allie were still crouched over the pile of kindling, aiming Allie's sunglasses at the last rays of waning light and blowing on a tiny plume of smoke, hoping the pile would magically burst into flame.

"Hey, Allie, catch," Skye chirped, tossing the box of waterproof matches.

Allie caught the box and shrieked when she realized what it contained. "Ohmuhgud, you rule!"

"Thanks," grinned Mel. "I didn't want to tell Al, but I'm not sure anyone's ever started a campfire with purple sunglasses."

"That's not all," Taz said, lugging the box of food and supplies down the stairs of the plane. "Skye found food and blankets. She pretty much saved us." His expression was still a little cool, but Skye could tell he was impressed.

"It was nothing," Skye blushed. Usually, if humility was called for, Skye had to fake it. But tonight, she was so relieved that Taz didn't hate her that she didn't have to fake a thing.

Their bellies full of canned chili and reconstituted mashed potatoes, the six castaways sat huddled around the fire pit, blankets draped over their shoulders, staring sleepily at the flames dancing high in the air. The cactus husks they'd piled in the pit crackled like Duraflame logs, sending pretty orange sparks into the ink-black, star-saturated desert sky. Skye leaned back and scanned the sky until she found the Big Dipper, her arm grazing Taz's foot in the process. Not such a terrible night at all, she found herself thinking. The only thing this camping trip lacked was a ride home when it was over.

"Camping like this reminds me of when we were kids," Darwin said over the pop-hiss of the fire. "We took a family trip to the Amazon rainforest with our mom when we were all really little. Mel, you must have been nine . . ."

"Eight," Mel corrected his little brother.

"Remember how she had the guide run ahead and plant relics among the stones of those old ruins? We thought we were Indiana Jones when we found them." Darwin smiled at the memory.

"*Your* mom did that?" Allie blurted, her navy blue eyes incredulous in the flickering firelight.

Skye looked from one Brazille-featured face to the next, glad she hadn't asked the question, but wondering the same thing. It was hard to imagine Shira doing something so sweet. The woman Darwin was describing bore no resemblance to the domineering, manipulative mogul Skye knew, who was all business and no fun, busy managing Alpha Island like it was her own personal dictatorship. Skye had just assumed she ran her family the same way.

Mel sat up, running a hand through his white-blond hair and shooting Allie a "lay off" look. "She's just . . . driven."

"Driven to torture us," Allie muttered under her breath.

Skye and Charlie giggled.

They each had their own reasons to hate Shira. She'd forced each girl to compromise herself so many times that none of the Jackie O's could fake understanding her, let alone liking her.

Even off-island, Shira had a way of showing up and dousing the fun. Finally, Taz interrupted the awkward silence hanging over the campfire. "Speaking of hiking trips, did I ever tell you about the guy I met on the slopes of Kilimanjaro?"

Skye studied Taz's profile as he launched into a creepy story about a strange man who'd walked with him up the mountain passes. His nose was aquiline, a perfect compliment to his high cheekbones and his cleft chin. His shiny black hair made his blue eyes that much more dramatic. But more than anything, Skye had always admired Taz's ability to work a room. To create a party out of nothing, and to have a good time no matter what. That was the kind of girl she'd been in Westchester. And Skye was starting to miss her.

Too bad the stress of competing against the most talented girls in the world, combined with Shira forcing her to continue a bogus relationship with Syd, had taken up so much of her energy.

But now that Taz didn't seem to truly hate her anymore—maybe she could be that girl again. The girl who put the fizz in the soda and the sparkle on the silver. Tonight, she felt the stirrings of the old Skye again, and with Taz spurring her on, maybe she would find a way to bring her back for keeps.

She blinked hard, forcing her attention back to what Taz was actually saying. Everyone else seemed completely enthralled.

"And that's when I realized, the guide *knew too much*. He was actually *the ghost of the dead explorer!*" Taz's hands waved in the air above the fire, forming spooky shadows against some nearby rocks.

Charlie: "Freaky."

Darwin: "No way."

Allie: "Yikers Island."

Mel (yawning): "Haven't we had enough terror for one day?"

Only Skye was enjoying being scared. Racing heart, tingling fingers, skin-crawling alertness; it felt like living. It felt like fun. A pleasantly creepy chill ran down her spine as she let herself get carried away by the ghost story. "So . . . what did you do?"

"I was freaking, you know, 'cause I like my friends to be . . . alive," Taz grinned. "So I knew it was him or me on that mountain . . ." He looked up suddenly. "Hey, what was that?"

Skye hadn't heard anything, but she'd spent enough summers at sleepaway camp to recognize a manufactured ghost at the end of a campfire story. Playing along, she tilted her head in mock fear to showcase her blond waves and light-reflecting cheekbones. "Ohmuhgod, I heard it, too!"

Then to her surprise, she actually *did* hear something; a creaking noise, followed by a weird dragging, crunching sound. It came from just behind the plane, or maybe from inside. Was Taz *that good*? Or was there some kind of wild desert animal sharpening his teeth on the metal, preparing to eat them while they slept? For all Skye knew, the desert was full of homicidal beasts waiting to bite into stranded teens. And these weren't any teens. They were Alphas. Grade A, free-range, organic, fat-free meals. She sat up straighter, opening her eyes wide and straining to listen to whatever was making the creepy noises.

"Dude, I thought you were joking!" Mel whisper-yelled, reaching over to punch his younger brother in the arm.

Taz looked more surprised and scared than anyone. "I was!" he mouthed.

The hairs on the back of Skye's neck stood on end. She jumped up from her seat and ran over to Charlie, grabbing her friend as the dragging sound continued. "What's going on?" she whispered.

"No idea," Charlie whisper-shrugged. "Maybe the PAP turned itself on. Let's go check it out."

"I'm coming with you." Darwin reached for an unused stick that lay next to the fire. Taz and Mel looked as freaked out as Skye felt, but Charlie, always brave and practical, stood up and flicked on her aPod to use as a flashlight. Skye swallowed a lump in her throat and stood up to follow them, trying to channel Indiana Jones. But as the creaking sound reached her ears again, a shiver ran down her spine that was straight out of *Saw*. She ran to catch up with the others, the fine blond hairs on her forearms standing up from fear.

So much for the fizz in the soda—at the moment Skye felt about as adventurous as tap water.

7

THE MOJAVE DESERT
BASE CAMP
NOVEMBER 2ND
8:48 P.M.

Allie lagged behind her fellow castaways, stress-Purelling and shivering in the cold night air. She wished she had thought of offering to stay behind and tending to the fire— wild animals just weren't her thing. She didn't even like touching cats! There was something about them she just didn't trust. Huddling close to Mel and Skye, she hoped whatever was behind the plane was gone now, or at least that it was friendly. She clamped a hand over her mouth to keep her Whitestrip-enhanced teeth from chattering—fear combined with the frigid desert night had turned her chompers into castanets.

The group pressed forward, heading toward the plane, when that same scratching sound reached Allie's goose-bumped ears. She grabbed Skye's toned upper arm and squeezed it in terror. "Did you hear that?"

Skye whirled around, the whites of her eyes glowing in the moonlight. "Ow! Let go of my arm."

But there it was again. This time, Skye heard it.

"Guys! It's that way!" Skye whisper-screamed and poked a thumb toward an outcropping of boulders just to the left of the plane.

Allie was too spooked to speak.

She ran behind Mel and cowered, holding onto his broad shoulders and burrowing her head into his back, though she wasn't sure what good it would do her. When they'd left the fire pit, Mel had grabbed a can opener from the mess kit they'd found on the plane. What was Mel planning to do, *open* the wolf to death? She rolled her navy blue eyes, annoyed that her boyfriend didn't have the sense to at least grab a stick and light it on fire. Everyone knew animals hated fire. Didn't they?

But just like her, Mel was more at home in a mall than he was in the wild. She peeked over his shoulder, standing on her tiptoes. Waiting was the worst part. *Let the fur fly and the carnage commence*, she thought. Anything beat going out of her mind with anticipation.

She braced herself for teeth. For snarling, for some kind of wild beast. Suddenly, she felt certain the animal would be a wolf. She tried to calm herself by thinking about how cute Taylor Lautner was in *Twilight: Eclipse*, but her teeth began to chatter again. She preferred her wolves onscreen, where they belonged: shirtless and sexy, not out here in this ice-cold, pitch-black kitty litter box, where they were more likely to have beady eyes, bad breath, claws, and an appetite.

Just then, something green and faintly fuzzy stirred behind the boulder nearest them.

"Hey." AJ appeared, her scratchy voice more grating than Parmesan. She hopped over a boulder to join the group, casually adjusting her green tam as if she'd bumped into them in the Alpha Pavilion.

Allie blinked. Had their chili been tainted? Was she hallucinating?

Ohmuhgod. An agonized groan escaped Allie's mouth before she clamped it shut with her hand. The group all stared at AJ with shocked expressions on their faces. Which meant that sadly, AJ wasn't just a vision of Allie's nightmares. She was the real thing.

Allie would have preferred a murderous wolf over this. Was there not anywhere on Earth that she could go to get away from the stinky songstress?

"What are you *doing* here?" Skye shrieked.

AJ aimed her seaweed-green eyes straight at Allie as a thin smile spread over her pointy face. She swallowed the remains of a BrazilleBlast bar she must have filched from the PAP. "You guys never include me in anything, so I decided to include myself," she said at last.

Allie looked at her friends, wrinkling her nose as a whiff of AJ's patchouli essential oil found its way into her airspace. "Am I having a nightmare, and you're all in it?"

Mel narrowed his pale green eyes. "You snuck onto the plane, you mean," he said coldly.

AJ stood blinking at the group, smiling calmly in spite of the angry silence hanging in the air. "Okay, yeah. I hid in one of the rear compartments. It wasn't so hard, if you haven't noticed, I'm tiny." AJ stretched her spindly arms out as though trying to prove it. "I heard you guys talking about the plan last night. I muted my aPod when I had my headphones on. I don't embrace the competitive spirit, but I felt like I should be a part of this experience." The words hung pointlessly in the air like a pair of old sneakers draped over a telephone wire.

"That is extremely weird," Darwin murmured, shaking his head.

"No big deal," AJ said brightly, her attitude maddeningly serene. "Why don't we all go back to the fire and chill out? Anyone up for a sing-a-long?" Before they could answer, she led the way.

At the fire, AJ threw a few sticks onto the blaze and plopped down to warm her hands, seemingly oblivious to the glares being shot at her from six still-incredulous sets of eyes.

Allie couldn't believe AJ had snuck onto the plane, but at least she wasn't a rabid animal or a deranged criminal hiding from the law. *That we know of.* The silent joke made Allie giggle.

Sighing as her sandaled feet began to thaw, Allie resolved not to let AJ being here get the best of her. There were way bigger threats to her safety now that they were stranded in the desert. What could the teeny greenie do to her out here? Allie leaned her head against Mel's shoulder and inhaled the scent of his Aveda sandalwood pomade. This whole thing was kind of romantic, if you looked at it the right way. Staring into the campfire, her beau beside her, Allie took on the character of a heroine in an old Western movie. If only Mel could ride her off into the sunset, or at least get the plane working.

She turned to look at her boyfriend and couldn't keep a tiny laugh from escaping her lips. His silver leggings and gauzy babydoll top didn't exactly fit the cowboy bill, but he was still a mega-hottie.

Allie began to brood over what tomorrow might bring. If Charlie couldn't fix the GPS and they couldn't alert anyone to their whereabouts, it was fully possible they'd all die out here. Allie began to imagine all the news stories that would run if the worst happened. The girls weren't celebrities, of course, but the Brazille boys had been on magazine covers for as long as Allie had known how to read. Their dramatic death would be covered everywhere—from *TMZ* to CNN. Her grieving parents would probably be on Oprah. The national tragedy would be almost on par with Princess Diana's death, or Marilyn Monroe's.

Allie shivered at the thought. Perversely, she began to picture her ex-boyfriend Fletcher and ex-bestie Trina cutting out her picture from all the papers, maybe even making a little shrine to Allie, whom they had betrayed by hooking up with each other on the Pirates of the Caribbean ride at Disneyland. They would blame themselves for her death, for hooking up and forcing a betrayed Allie to join Alpha Academy to forget about them. Hopefully, word would get out that Allie died the girlfriend of Mel Brazille, who topped Fletcher in every way possible.

She turned to Mel again, but his back was to her this time as he nodded vigorously, engrossed in conversation with . . . *huh?*

AJ sat on the other side of Mel, and he pushed his white-blond hair off his forehead and nodded in agreement with something the jolly green midget had just said. "I know what you mean about playing music. Modeling is the same way. Once I finally got over stage fright and was fully confident in myself, that's when my modeling really took off."

"Exactly," AJ drawled, meeting his eyes with her faux-earnest gaze. "The audience trusts you when you trust yourself."

Allie's navy blue eyes shot skyward while her face burned with jealousy. How dare AJ try to bond with Mel by recycling stale self-help clichés! She was lucky to get a BrazilleBlast bar and a warm spot by the fire—no way was she going to monopolize Allie's boyfriend.

"I feel exactly the same way about acting," Allie piped up, attempting to join the conversation.

"No offense," AJ sneered, a stray lock of her dyed-black hair escaping her crusty green tam, "but didn't you just start acting, like, three weeks ago? It takes years to get comfortable onstage. You wouldn't really under-stand—"

"Of course she would," Mel laughed. "Have you seen this girl act? She's a scene stealer."

Take that!

"Yeah, Allie's always been quite good at impersonating others." AJ tossed her stringy, awapuhi-cleansed locks and turned toward Charlie and Darwin.

Allie grinned as she nuzzled her cheek against the crook of Mel's beefy shoulder, not even caring that it was clothed in a poly-blend boatneck shirt. Mel wasn't just perfect, he was loyal. Which was even more important to Allie, especially after what she'd been through with Fletcher and Trina.

So Mel didn't wrangle a horse out of thin air and whisk her off into the sunset—he had just proven there were other ways to rescue a damsel in distress.

8

THE MOJAVE DESERT
BASE CAMP
NOVEMBER 3RD
7:10 A.M.

Charlie blinked awake in time to catch the most striking pink-and-orange sunrise she'd ever seen. And considering she'd seen the sunrise from every continent, that was saying a lot. Peeling back the thin silver blanket that covered her, Skye, and a still-asleep Darwin, she sat up and stared at the vibrant Kool-Aid-colored sky, a relaxed smile on her chapped lips.

Even after spending the night on the hard ground, waking up with the sun felt natural and peaceful, like she'd been transported back to a prehistoric time, to a simpler world where people didn't worry about text messages or toilet paper. Her smile deepened when she thought about how much fun it was to sit around the campfire with her friends last night. Even though she was totally freaked out and half freezing to death, she had never just hung out with friends like this before. No pressure, no agendas, just real. Maybe she wanted this more than she wanted to be an Alpha. She ran her fingers through her long brown hair, picking a few twigs from what she hoped wasn't a hopeless rat's nest acquired after her night spent sandwiched between Darwin and Skye on the desert floor.

Careful not to wake the others, Charlie crawled out from her space in the middle of the sleeping castaways. There were only a few blankets on the plane, so everyone had wound up pressed together like a litter of piglets burrowing for warmth. Charlie's sleep-puffed eyes found the fire pit, where the blaze had burned down to a few weak embers. AJ slept closest to it, slightly removed from the group and curled in a tight ball. She wore her green tam pulled down over her eyes like a sleep mask, and in the night it had become even filthier than usual, dotted with dried leaves and ash from the fire. *Gross.*

Darwin was stirring. He smacked his full lips like he was dreaming of pancakes, then turned over and caught a few more Zs. The rest of the downed crew slept on peacefully. The boys were still in their girly outfits, and Charlie swallowed a giggle when she noticed Taz's (shaved) legs sticking out from the bottom of his blanket. A pair of silver platform heels lay tossed at his feet. The scene looked more like the aftermath of a bachelor party than a plane crash.

Charlie tiptoed to survey the landscape in the soft morning light. Other than the tall saguaro cacti dotting the beige earth like cowboys waving both hands in the air, the only other signs of life came from clouds moving fast across the brightening sky.

She sniffed the air, which smelled of sage and dust and the dying embers of the campfire. This was the first moment of real peace Charlie could remember. Now that Alpha Island's pressure-cooker atmosphere had boiled over into a winner-take-all war, Charlie's stress levels had been boiling over, too.

For a split second, she fantasized about what it would be like to live out here forever. If only they could find a water source, Charlie wouldn't mind waking up with the sun each day. As long as Darwin and her friends could stay, too. With him sleeping by her side under the stars, Charlie was pretty sure they wouldn't miss civilization at all.

But just when Charlie had begun to feel like this real-life Georgia O'Keeffe painting was exactly where she was supposed to be, her sense of inner peace was shattered by the shrill cries of three birds circling about a hundred feet away from the campsite. Their black, feathered bodies hung high in the air, but their prehistoric call was unmistakable—*buzzards*.

Ohmuhgud. Didn't buzzards only circle like this when death was imminent? Charlie's tranquility evaporated, instantly morphing back into her familiar anxiety. Unless she figured out how to get a signal to radio for help, they'd be bird turds by this time tomorrow. Her stomach lurched with worry as she bent down and started gathering sticks and twigs, her hands clawing at the dusty brown floor of the desert. They needed to keep the fire lit in case a plane came. Once she had gathered a few handfuls of kindling, she would head back to tackle the broken GPS.

Narrowing her hazelnut eyes to scan the ground for cactus husks and dried seedpods, Charlie's thoughts drifted to the person who had become her primary stress-inducer this year: Shira. What would the obnoxious Aussie do if Charlie died out here, in the American version of the outback?

Shira was famous for clawing her way to the top and staying there because she always looked out for number one. One of her mottos was "no regrets," but regret was exactly what she would feel if Charlie and the others died. Regret, and maybe even guilt. Because in a way, this was all Shira's fault. If she hadn't turned her prestigious academy into a shark tank where every day might be an Alpha's last, the girls would never have been driven to attempt insane competitions like this PAP race.

And Shira had extra reason to feel guilty about Charlie. She'd made Charlie's mom, Bee, her loyal assistant for thirteen years, quit her job in exchange for Charlie's enrollment in the Academy. Not to mention forcing Charlie to dump Darwin, which had made her first few months here the most emotionally taxing of her life. Now, all because of Shira's vague announcement that one Alpha would prove herself a leader and become an AFL (Alpha for life), Charlie had risked everything. Charlie let out a choked sigh of frustration. Just thinking about Shira elevated her heart rate.

If Charlie died, Shira would surely set up a foundation in her name. Young girls could compete—Shira loved competition, after all—for the Charlie Deery scholarship. And Shira would have to live with the guilt of her death for the rest of her long, cryogenically prolonged life. There was a tiny bit of malicious pleasure Charlie could take in that fact.

But what about Bee? She'd given up her career with Shira so Charlie could have the best education on Earth. Was *this* how Charlie was going to repay her? By dying pointlessly in the desert? Charlie froze as she answered her own question, her hands clutching a bouquet of twigs so hard that several snapped in half. *No freaking way.*

She had worked too hard at the Academy and given up too much for all of it to end out here. Charlie squeezed her eyes shut so hard that purple spots swam across her closed lids. Then she opened them wide. The only thing she'd regret was giving up.

She hurried back to the campfire and threw the kindling into the embers before quietly making her way back over to the PAP, where she took the plane's stairs two at a time and hopped into the cockpit. Charlie was one of the best inventor-tracked Alphas in school, wasn't she? Hadn't she

73

created a whole fleet of mechanical butterflies and a tele-portational travel system that had the potential to change the world? Hadn't she patented a chemical compound for mood-glow nail polish that changed colors based on the wearer's emotional state, and hadn't mood-glow nail polish already netted Brazille Industries millions of dollars in sales? Charlie wasn't one to dwell on her accomplishments, but today she needed to remind herself of just how much she was capable of achieving.

Compared with all that, a broken GPS module should be cake. She smiled, turning the silver capsule-shaped GPS over in her hands. She just needed to treat it like her rela-tionships—sometimes things needed to come apart before they could work again.

Charlie spotted one of Allie's bobby pins on the floor of the plane's backseat and used it to fashion a makeshift screwdriver. She unscrewed the flat silver panel on the back of the shiny GPS module. The inside of the device con-sisted of a motherboard, several multicolored wires, and a larger white wire that led to a flat, cylindrical battery unit. Maybe if she opened up the big white wire and rebraided the copper inside, she could jump-start the battery and the extra juice would force the machine to find a signal. Seemed like as good a plan as any.

Working slowly, Charlie hummed a Katy Perry song that Taz had played last night as she stripped the wire.

The campsite was beginning to buzz with yawns and conversation—the rest of the crew had woken up, which meant that soon, Charlie would have to tell them they still didn't have a way out of here. She shook her head slightly, tuning out the sound of Taz and Skye flirting, the sound of Allie complaining about having to pee on a cactus, and the sound of AJ moaning about how loud they all were.

Come on, Charlie whispered to the GPS as she plugged the rejiggered wire back into the battery pack. *Give me a little juice to go with breakfast, why don't you?*

With shaking hands, Charlie flipped the switch on the side of the GPS unit to ON. For a moment, the pill-shaped device buzzed from the power boost and Charlie thought she'd done it. But then the motherboard flew out of its slot, leaving the wires exposed and crackling with blue sparks, and it was everything Charlie could do not to cry.

She sealed her eyes shut and bit her lower lip to keep the tears back. *Crying won't get you home.* When she opened them again and sat back in the white leather pilot's seat, she stared down at the mess she'd created: a million little pieces of GPS littering the ground.

"Hey." Charlie looked up to see Darwin's head just a few feet from hers, peering at her through the open window of the cockpit. Allie was with him, her brow furrowed with concern. How long had he and Allie had been watching her stare into space?

Charlie wanting to smile reassuringly at Darwin, but barely managed a limp grin. "Hi."

Darwin smiled for both of them.

"Still no luck, huh?" Allie piped up cheerfully. A sympathetic frown alighted on her rosebud mouth for a moment.

"I think I made it worse," Charlie whispered, swallowing another round of frustrated tears. "I don't know when we're getting out of here, guys. I thought maybe if I jump-started the battery . . ." she trailed off, not wanting to bother explaining her latest scheme since it had failed anyway.

"So, um, I had an idea. It came to me just as I was waking up," Allie said, her ski-slope nose wrinkling as she flashed Charlie an *I've-got-this* kind of look.

Charlie shrugged and stared at her hands folded on her lap. Allie was sweet to try and think of something, but the girl didn't know a mascara wand from a data stick. There was no way someone with zero engineering knowledge could fix this.

"Charlie, hear her out," Darwin said softly, sensing her hesitation.

Charlie forced a nod and turned her bloodshot eyes toward Allie. If Darwin was insisting, maybe Allie had an idea worth listening to. "Let's hear it," she said weakly.

"Okay, so I know you guys didn't watch a lot of TV when you were traveling the world, but on *LOST*, there's a plane

76

crash, and the survivors have to hike to the highest peak on the island to get a radio signal."

"Uh huh," Charlie said, waiting for the idea.

Allie widened her navy blue eyes and tilted her head as if Charlie were being dense. "So . . . maybe if we find the tallest plateau in the desert, there's a chance our GPS or our aPods will pick something up."

Charlie considered the possibility. Static was all the GPS was able to produce down here, but maybe Allie had something. Maybe they were in some kind of dead zone, and a signal would find its way to their many electronic devices if they left it. Nothing else had worked.

"I think it's worth a try," Darwin said. "What do you say, Charlie?"

Fitting the pieces of the broken GPS back together like a high-stakes Rubik's cube, Charlie shot a quick glance at the whitening sky. The buzzards were circling lower now.

"I say it's more than worth it. Let's get going."

9

THE MOJAVE DESERT
ROAD TO FREEDOM
NOVEMBER 3
9:17 A.M.

Over the past hour, Skye's lower half had gone from supple to cement. She brought up the rear, lagging behind her fellow hikers as they trudged in a winding, dusty line toward the top of the first plateaued mountain they'd spotted. The climb grew steeper by the minute, and Skye paused to take a sip from her A-shaped canteen. Swallowing and flattening her parched lips into a determined line, she used all her dancer's willpower to force her legs to keep walking. If feet had mouths, hers would be swearing. And Skye's spirits sagged even lower than her arches.

Not that the rest of the group looked much better. At the front of the death march, Charlie and Darwin led the way. They stared straight ahead as they walked, steely and determined, too tired for conversation. Next came Allie and Mel: chattier, slower, and way more annoying. Mel's arm was permanently draped around Allie's slim shoulders, and in the mirage-inducing sunlight they looked like a two-headed metallic beast lurching through across the broiling surface of Mars. Even AJ seemed to be faring better than Skye. She shuffled along to the side of the group humming, looking up now and again to shoot menacing glances at Allie. But at least she was moving at a steady pace.

"That's *it*," Skye finally yelled, stopping to pick up a jagged rock from along the desert path, and aiming it directly at her flight suit.

"Skye, no!" Allie cried. "It's not too late, we can still get out of here!"

Skye shook her head with a laugh. "I'm not trying to hurt myself, Al." She rubbed the rock against the metallic fabric's edge, making a big gash in the material. Then she began to rip. "I'm . . . just . . . so . . . HOT." With a grunt, Skye yanked the remaining cloth from her jacket. In the one-shoulder top that remained, she now looked more like a gilded Amazonian than a PAP pilot. "What?" she said in response to the group's curious expressions. "I grew up in leotards and shrugs my entire life. We had to get creative if we wanted to look fabulous. Who's next?"

Moments later, each one of the girls strode along the desert floor looking more like Lara Croft than Jackie O. But Skye could have been butt-naked and still would have felt like she was walking through a wood-fire pizza oven. She staggered over a few large rocks, cursing her clear gladiator sandals for their lack of traction. If anyone was going to drop first, it was definitely going to be her. She looked longingly at a shriveled desert shrub clinging to the side of a rock, thinking about how ah-mazing it would be to rest her head in the six-inch patch of shade beneath it and never get up.

Her parents would eventually find her sun-bleached skeleton, and they would fly her remains back for a huge memorial service in Westchester. All her old friends from OCD would come, dressed in designer black suits their mothers let them buy to honor the tragedy. Her own mother, Natasha Flailenkoff, beautiful former prima ballerina and owner of Body Alive Dance Studio, would mourn her only daughter in a beautiful, dramatic, Russian style. She'd probably gild a pair of Skye's toe shoes and hang them in the studio for all the little tutu'd girls to aspire to . . .

Well, screw that! Skye rubbed her temples and shook her aching head to erase the morbid fantasy from her mind. Her toe shoes would hang in Lincoln Center someday, not in Body Alive Dance Studio off the Saw Mill Parkway.

She executed a quick *en pointe* to remind herself that she was still a living, breathing ballet dancer, arching the blistered soles of her feet and throwing her chest forward as her arms swept upward in two perfect semi-circles. She still had a lot of work to do on this Earth, and a stupid plane crash wasn't going to erase her twelve years of dance training. Jutting her sunburned chin out in front of her, Skye straightened her posture and picked up the pace.

The one member of the group she kept losing sight of was Taz. For the past hour, he'd been darting in and out of the of the scrubby desert bushes with newfound objects (A quartz crystal! A sandstone that looks exactly like Stewie from *Family Guy*!) and observations (My B.O. is way less funky than Mel's! I think I can see Burning Man from here!). Now he came crashing into sight from behind a sage plant, still wearing his pleated skirt and white Alphas blouse. He stuck out his tongue and pointed to a saliva-coated purple leaf. Skye didn't know whether to laugh or gag.

"Want one?" Taz grinned. "Sage leaves help prevent dehydration. Learned about it a couple years ago on safari."

"Sure." Skye plucked a grayish leaf from Taz's outstretched hand and popped it in her mouth, her heart suddenly racing. Whenever she was around Taz, she felt as if she'd drunk about eighteen cups of green tea without the peeing part. Every molecule of her body felt alive and energized, and it wasn't the sage leaf. It was Taz's infectious energy.

Even now, he bounded up the trail like he was born to hike in 100-degree heat. She pushed herself to match his pace, trying not to pant like a sled dog. She'd do whatever it took to keep up with Taz. He must feel the same way, right? Skye tried to figure out what was going through his mind as they passed AJ along the path.

Her eyes focused on Taz's pleated silver skirt ahead of her, Skye thought back to last night, when she found the food. He told her she was awesome. But then he'd high-fived her. Did boys only high-five their friends? He'd given her the sage leaf just now, but apparently he'd gathered up a lot of them, because now he was handing them out to Mel and Allie.

Skye blinked, realizing she had lost sight of Taz again as the path bent around a boulder. The sun was blindingly bright already, and for a second all she saw was heat ripples in front of her. She stopped in front of the boulder, unsure which way to go.

"Up here," came Taz's voice. Skye looked up and saw the shadow of her cross-dressed crush standing on top of the rock, blocking out the sun behind him. He opened his strong arms out wide à la DiCaprio in *Titanic*, stuck his chest out and shouted "I'm freeeee!"

Skye's heart sunk again. *So free you don't need me.*

"Sorry," he called down, blushing a little. "I'm just so happy to be off that island, out of my mom's sight!"

Taz was obviously too happy flying solo to care whether she was his girlfriend or not. He jumped off the boulder and kept walking up the mountain, leaving Skye to shake her head and follow.

But the longer she walked, the more Skye realized she didn't care. If she was going to die out here, she didn't want to do it with any regrets. She wanted her last few days of life to mean something. She wanted them to be crazy and energetic and . . . Taz-esque.

She ran to catch up with him, forcing her legs and arms to propel her through the sauna-hot air.

"I have a game we can play," she announced, trying to make her voice sound as confident as possible.

"Nice!" Taz said. "I think I've run out of ideas."

"What happened to being *free?*" Skye said playfully.

"I am free," he shot back with a smirk. "I'm also bored."

Taz wiped a long bead of sweat from his cheek. His light blue eyes were playful, completely devoid of the hate-daggers she'd felt directed at her so many times over the past weeks.

Skye's chest thumped. It felt like her heart was punching her ribs, like her body was ordering her to make the next move. She glanced ahead to where the others were still trekking in the distance. If they didn't pick up the pace, they might lose them. But she didn't care. She had to find out how Taz felt.

"Okay, the game is Would You Rather: Alpha Edition," she said. "Ready?"

"Hit me," Taz replied.

"Would you rather shave your legs for the rest of your life, or never cut your hair again?" Skye asked.

"Hair," Taz said without hesitating. "This leg thing is

brutal. Plus, I'd look pretty cool with long locks." He smiled, tossing a fake mane. "Like Tarzan." He banged his fists on his chest and let out a jungle call.

"Okay," Skye smiled and rolled her eyes, then thought hard. "Would you rather live with your mother until you are married, or never get to make fun of your brothers again?"

Taz thought a little harder about this one. "I guess I'd live with my mother," he said finally. "I mean, she's not always so bad. And have you met my brothers? They were born asking for it."

Taz was good at this game. But Skye still had one more question she needed to ask . . .

Here goes nothing.

She took a deep breath, pasting on her most professional stage smile. "Would you rather date any other girl on Alpha Island . . ." Skye bit her lip. ". . . or me?" Her words hung in the dry air like a white flag of surrender. She'd barely spoken the last part out loud, but she knew he'd heard her. She held her breath, waiting to see if Taz would take the bait or signal that the war wasn't over.

Taz slowed his pace to a stop and stared down at a prickly cactus as though it held the answers he needed. Skye looked at the desert floor, too, nervously turning her toes from first to second position and back again. Then she glanced back at Taz. It was weird to see him so thoughtful. Or was his expression angry? Skye began to panic. What if he was about to tell her—again!—that there was no way he wanted anything to do with her? How could she force her legs to keep walking after that kind of rejection? Where could she go to hide? They were in the middle of the desert. Talk about awkward.

Just when Skye's brain was about to implode with anxiety, Taz looked at her. That's when she realized his eyes were full of hurt. "That depends," he said softly. "Would you also be dating my brother?"

Skye could almost hear her heart shattering, like a rose dipped in dry ice in eighth-grade chemistry class.

"Actually, I wanted to explain that whole thing," Skye rushed to fill the chilly silence between them with words, starting carefully as she tried to explain why she'd given Syd a chance in the first place. But pretty soon, her halting recollection of how Syd had charmed her with poetry became a rushed explanation of everything that had happened and before she knew it, Skye was finally explaining to Taz why she had no choice but to keep dating Syd in spite of knowing the better choice was him.

"I realized my mistake a long time ago," Skye said, staring at Taz's scraped kneecaps below the hem of his metallic pleated skirt instead of his light blue eyes. "Syd was never right for me. It was you all along."

"Then you should have ended things with him instead of leading him on," Taz said with an edge in his voice.

"I was just about to end things," Skye couldn't help her voice from sounding irritated. "But then your mom got involved."

Taz blinked hard in surprise. "Huh?"

Skye risked another peek at her crush's face. His mouth was twisted in anger, but his thick eyebrows were raised in curiosity. "My mom played a part in this?" Then, quieter, he mumbled something else. "Why does that not surprise me?"

Skye shrug-sighed. "Shira told me that if I broke Syd's heart, she would break my enrollment. It was either stay with Syd or leave Alpha Island."

There, now he knows the whole truth. She sucked on the sage leaf still in her mouth, ran a hand nervously along the bumps in her blond bun and waited. All she could do now was hope he'd understand.

But maybe he wouldn't get it, Skye's inner pessimist argued. Taz didn't know what it was like to have to fight for stuff. Growing up as Shira's son meant he'd never had to. Then again, her inner optimist pointed out, he definitely noticed (and hated) the way Shira controlled everyone around her. That much was clear from the way he'd acted after the plane crash. Her teal eyes searched his to try to figure out how he was processing her bombshell.

"So *that's* why you acted so weird to Syd," Taz mused. He smacked his forehead, and a lock of his shiny black hair fell adorably over his left eye. "You were trying to get him to dump you."

"Exactly!" Skye burst out, happy that Taz made the mental leap so she wouldn't have to spell everything out in excruciating—and embarrassing—detail. She didn't feel like reliving her faux-farts, greasy hair, or onion breath. Not when she was trying to get Taz to consider her date-able again. "My only hope was to be as gross and weird as I could, so Syd would move on and get obsessed with . . . I mean get interested in . . . some other girl," Skye giggle-shrugged.

"News flash. You weren't that good at it." Taz's eyes sparkled mischievously. He plucked a little white flower off a lethal-looking cactus and twirled it in Skye's direction.

"At what?" Skye put her hands on her narrow hips. Was Taz really going to dredge up the past and make her relive how painful it was to be trapped in a lie with Syd, and then start immediately making fun of her for it? She was all for gentle teasing, especially after what she'd put him through, but telling her she sucked was just . . . mean. Skye instinctively rolled her shoulders back to ease the tension in her body as she wondered if Taz was more trouble than he was worth. Better to keep on being single and fighting to become top Alpha than to put up with this.

"You aren't very good at making people stop liking you."

Taz stared at her pointedly, a flicker of a smile slowly turning into a goofy grin on his handsome face.

Wait, what?

And then it hit Skye, the realization as sharp and acute as an elbow jab to the ribs. He still liked her!

She threw her head back and laughed, not her normal nervous Taz-manian giggle but a real, happy peal of laughter, because it was finally obvious that Taz was into her again. The brutally bright sunlight momentarily blinded her and when she finished laughing and directed her gaze back at him, all she could see was the dark outline of his face.

Specifically, his lips. Just a couple of inches away from her own. Now she *really* didn't care if they ever caught up with the others again.

Ohmuhgud. Skye shut off her head and let her heart be her choreographer.

Suddenly, even on this dry, dusty patch of desert, she felt weightless, like she was submerged underwater. Her face tilted sideways as her body leaned in. Every particle of her wanted to collide with the dark-haired, blue-eyed boy in front of her, and now she knew he felt the same way.

And then Taz kissed her, his lips the one soft thing in the prickly, hard Mojave desert. His arms pulled her flight-suited shoulders close, and she didn't even have time to wonder how gross and sweaty she felt. She held on to him, too, her body suddenly light enough to float away like a balloon. Skye wasn't thinking about getting rescued anymore. Sure, an airdropped crate of toiletries, fresh clothes, and clean linens would be nice, but that was no longer necessary. The kiss was saving her.

10

THE MOJAVE DESERT
TOP OF THE PLATEAU
NOVEMBER 3RD
10:06 A.M.

Charlie was good at pretending. She could pretend to respect the way Shira ran her Academy. She could shrug her shoulders and play dumb when asked how the island's surveillance system got broken. She could even pretend that Darwin looked cute during his blessedly short-lived emo phase when he dyed his naturally highlighted hair blue-black.

But at some point, even the best pretenders dropped their masks. Charlie's mask hung by a thread thinner than dental floss, and any minute now that thread was going to break.

For hours, she'd been pretending to be strong and upbeat as she led seven exhausted, dehydrated, and ridiculously dressed Alphas and Brazilles up the side of a searing-hot mountain devoid of shade. Soon it would be noon. The sun's heat would only grow hotter, she had a huge painful blister under her gladiator sandals, and she was down to less than half a canteen of water.

In other words, if the GPS didn't work, they were screwed. And all the pretending in the world wasn't going to help Charlie hide it from her friends. Aside from AJ, who stumbled along the rocky terrain humming to herself, they were a smart, perceptive group. They'd know something was up.

Charlie knew Darwin could see it, too. Charlie's exhaustion hung on her like a heavy coat, dragging her down with each thudding, blister-rubbing step. Darwin kept walking doggedly at her side, his own foot bleeding where the strap of a too-small pair of platform sandals dug into his skin.

"We're here!" Mel shouted up ahead. Somehow, he had found the energy to push ahead of Charlie and Darwin to climb over the last boulders that led to the mountaintop, where a wide, circular plateau awaited them. Mel dropped to his legging-covered knees and actually kissed the dusty ground as Allie clambered up the boulders and looked on with a weirded-out expression on her dust-streaked face.

As Charlie and Darwin struggled up the rocks to join them, Charlie could hear Taz still playing the "What would you do for a bite of food" game with AJ and Skye. She had one unopened BrazilleBlast bar left, but Charlie had kept it hidden, wedged into her pack along with the GPS. They'd need it soon enough.

Taz's game was getting a little out of hand. *He must be really hungry*, Charlie thought as she scrambled up a boulder and turned to watch the stragglers approach. "But would you eat a scorpion, uncooked?" he asked, breathing hard as he helped push an exhausted Skye ahead of him.

"Yeah, I would," Skye said, her eyes visibly rolling under her gold aviators.

"Would you bludgeon it to death, or throw it on a fire and burn it alive?" Taz asked.

"Stop!" AJ squealed, bringing up the rear. "As a member of PETA, I insist you find another game."

"As a member of humanity I insist you find a sense of humor," Allie shot back.

When she finally reached the plateau, Charlie's legs collapsed beneath her. She sank to the ground like a wind sock minus the wind.

Now comes the moment of truth. Charlie shrugged her metallic mini-backpack off her sweaty shoulders and unzipped it. She pulled out their aPods and the GPS module, laying everything in front of her on the ground so everyone could see what she was working with. Or *not* working with, as the case may be.

"Go higher, Charles," Allie said. Charlie turned and saw Allie's freshly Purelled thumb gesturing to a giant, flat-topped rock. "That's the highest point around."

"Fine," Charlie shrugged.

"I'm coming, too," Darwin said, grabbing the GPS and limping over to the boulder.

On top of the boulder, with Darwin bent over the GPS unit, Charlie felt like she might panic-puke. *Be calm . . .* she commanded herself. *Don't rush this.* She pulled Allie's bobby pin out of a small zippered pocket on the arm of her flight suit and gestured for Darwin to hand over the GPS unit.

"What are you doing? Don't you want to try turning it on?" he said, holding the GPS tightly against his chest.

"I want to check the motherboard and make sure all the wires look okay before we risk blowing out the unit," Charlie answered, hoarse with exhaustion. She had rushed when she fit all the pieces back together, and she needed to check her work. *Please*, her cocoa-brown eyes pleaded with him. *I'm too tired to fight.*

"I think we should try it first. If it doesn't work, we can always open it back up," Darwin started, but Charlie had already heard enough.

"No." She shook her head and snatched the GPS angrily from his hands. "I can't believe you don't trust me enough to let me do this right," she muttered. "Who's the engineer, Darwin? Me or you?"

Darwin's hazel eyes flashed with momentary anger that quickly dissolved into hurt. "Fine. Sorry for trying to help. Let's do it your way."

Charlie nodded silently, blinking away tears of frustration. She knew she'd snapped, but she was mad, too, hurt
that Darwin would try to tell her how to do something she
knew so much more about than he did. But right now she
had a job to do. She would save the anger for later. If there
was even going to *be* a later.

Charlie looked down at the machine, unscrewing the
cover with shaking hands. Then she felt Darwin's hand on
her chin, tilting her face up to his.

"I'm sorry," he said, his mouth forming a tentative
let's-make-up smile. "No matter what, you'll always be my
angelfish. Don't forget that."

Angelfish. Of course he went there. Because when it
came down to it, Darwin knew exactly how to make her feel
better. Charlie's mouth uncurled from a stressed-out pucker
as she let her thoughts travel back to the coast of Brazil,
where three years ago Darwin had first told her how much
he cared about her. They were practically kids still, sitting
on the edge of a snorkeling boat that Shira had chartered.
Everyone else was either already in the water or working
on one of Shira's documentaries when their Brazilian boat
captain pointed out a school of angelfish below.

"*Pez angel.* They mate for life," the captain said. "*Muy
romantico.*"

Darwin had blushed a deep red, and when the captain
turned away, he grabbed Charlie's hand and whispered that

he was pretty sure she was his angelfish. Then he'd jumped into the water. When he surfaced, the school of angelfish had scattered, but Darwin's goofy smile made Charlie even happier than the fish could.

Charlie and Darwin had never forgotten that moment. They'd even talked about getting matching angelfish tattoos someday. Charlie looked up at him and wordlessly leaned over to give him a crushing hug, using the last of her strength. Darwin hugged her back, his breath reassuring and warm against her brown hair.

Suddenly the GPS flicked to life. Their hug must have activated it!

"Darwin!" Charlie cried, pulling away from him to stare down at the machine. Instead of static, there was a real, clear radio signal.

"It's working!" Darwin cheered. He stood up from the boulder and nearly fell off as he yelled to the others. "Guys, we got a signal!"

Charlie grinned and turned to give the rest of the crew a thumbs-up, but they were all looking at something else. And screaming. And flapping their arms. Allie stood stock-still in the center of the plateau, her mouth a perfect O, her arms in the air. Next to her, Taz was screaming while doing the moonwalk. Mel was on the ground doing snow angels in the dust, his silver legging-encased legs flailing. What was going on?

Charlie whirled around to see what it was behind her that had gotten everyone's attention, not daring to hope for a plane. But when her eyes met the sky, she saw that was exactly what it was.

"That was fast," Darwin said as a shiny blimp floated toward them. Definitely not your average Delta flight to Delaware, but hey, it would work. And it was coming closer.

Waving her arms and screaming louder than the front row of a Justin Bieber concert, Charlie almost sobbed with relief. Darwin grabbed her shoulders and spun her around, and the two of them jumped up and down together, hugging hard enough to crush each other's windpipes but not caring in the least.

Now their version of forever wouldn't end in the desert. In fact, Charlie realized as the plane got closer, forever might actually be a long, long time. Thank goodness. Because these two angelfish had a lot more swimming to do.

11

THE MOJAVE DESERT
TOP OF THE PLATEAU
NOVEMBER 3RD
10:15 A.M.

Shocked into statue-caliber stillness in the center of the plateau, Allie dared to breathe a tentative sigh of relief as the plane flew closer. Soon, the sigh became a whoop of joy and relief. They were saved!

Ever since they'd spotted the plane, they'd all been waving and screaming like a bunch of Beliebers in the nosebleed seats of a stadium show. Now that they knew the plane saw them, too, every sunburned pair of shoulders visibly relaxed as the odd-looking aircraft slowed above them, hovering for a moment before lowering forty, then thirty, then twenty feet above the seven exhausted castaways.

Allie's navy blue eyes squinted hard even beneath her purple sunglasses, but she was too tired to obsess about crow's feet and too curious not to stare. The plane's huge propeller whirred noisily, and in seconds, there was so much sand in the air that Allie could hardly see her hand in front of her face. She pressed her forearms over her fore-head and eyes, leaving just a slit to see from, and began to look for Mel. At six feet and 175 pounds, her boyfriend would make a much better windshield than her arms ever could.

She ran blindly around the plateau, coughing as dust filled her lungs, before at last she crashed into Mel. "This way," he screamed over the sound of the propeller, and they ran together toward the edge of the plateau and waited for the sand to settle.

While the plane slowly lowered to the ground, Allie lifted her face out from under Mel's girly lace shrug and examined their ride home through the curtain of beige dust it had kicked up. The plane was entirely platinum, as if it had been dipped in high-quality metal. Even the windows were tinted.

It was really more of a blimp than a plane, except it had those huge propellers and was designed with an indentation in the middle that gave it a kind of waist, like a curvy girl wearing a tight belt or a sparkling sky peanut.

"Get back!" Darwin hollered in a hoarse voice. He shoved Mel hard in the chest, and Mel grabbed Allie's hand and pulled her with him to give the plane a wider landing pad.

With a sound like a thousand ionic blow-dryers blasting all at once, the peanut-craft lowered down and four little legs popped out of its body so it appeared to be squatting on the ground.

A crazy-lady laugh escaped Allie's dry lips, partly in response to the bizarre-looking plane, but mostly she laughed from relief. The desert was dirty and desolate. Sure it was kind of cool to feel so tiny in such a big landscape, but she could go to Zara and try on all the size twelves to get the same rush.

As their rescue became more and more imminent, Allie grabbed Mel's hand and squeezed. Whatever happened— they'd probably be kicked out by Shira the second she found out they'd crashed the PAP—at least she could go home feeling good about how things had ended for her here. After all, she had come a long way from the girl who'd snuck in by posing as someone else. She'd gotten over Fletcher, at least as much as she ever would. She had found a possible soul mate in Mel, who happened to be one of the most coveted celeb-utantes alive. She had also found her passion in acting, and she believed in herself enough to pursue it seriously.

And most of all, she'd found Charlie and Skye. Allie was absolutely certain they'd stay friends for life. If a plane crash didn't bond you, nothing would. Allie blinked hard, dislodging a layer of desert crud from her long eyelashes. She looked from Mel on her right to Charlie, Darwin, and Skye standing to her left, and her heart swelled like it had just been injected with collagen.

LISI HARRISON

"I love you guys!" Allie shouted. But the thousand-watt blow-dryer hum blocked anyone from hearing. Then a thought bounced toward the negative like a pinball shot out with a flipper. *And I don't want this all to end!* If only they could fly back to Alpha Island and not be met with the sight of their packed suitcases and a one-way ticket to the real world.

As if she could read her friend's thoughts, Charlie moved closer to Allie and gave her tan shoulders a squeeze. "Hey, we're saved," her friend's voice said in her ear. "I'd rather be alive and expelled than dead and still an Alpha, wouldn't you?"

"Yeah," Allie shook her head. "I just wish this wasn't about to end. It doesn't feel over."

"What?" Charlie shouted over the roar of the plane's whirling propellers.

Allie nodded her head so Charlie could tell that yes, she'd rather be alive to face another day than dead in a metallic flight suit.

Finally, the propellers stopped whirring. The platinum peanut had landed atop the plateau, dust settling around its insect legs.

Taz and Skye bolted up to the golden nose of the plane and started wiping away the layer of dust now coating the space where the windows should have been. They ran around the side and pulled open a small portal to the cockpit. Skye and Taz stuck their heads in, then pulled them out, looking perplexed. Their hands dropped to their sides.

"There's nobody driving!" Skye yelled, waving her hands in agitated confusion. "It's empty."

Just then, the plane's engine went silent. A perfectly round door in the center of the plane's side popped open, and a ladder soon followed, bending and extending to the ground like a single leg of a golden caterpillar.

"It must be remotely operated," Charlie said, suspicion replacing relief in her big brown eyes. "Why would a remotely operated aircraft show up here? I don't get it."

"Who cares, we're saved!" Allie interrupted. Couldn't they just be happy for five minutes? Charlie always overthought things. The analytical part of her brain was set on perma-worry. Obviously, there weren't any other options, so they may as well take what they had. She turned to embrace Mel, determined to celebrate the fact that even if they were expelled, at least they weren't destined to turn into sun-bleached skeletons.

But when she whirled around on one blistered, gladiator-sandaled foot, Mel's beefy body was nowhere in sight. He had vanished, leaving only a view of beige desert landscape in his place. Allie frowned, her eyes scanning the empty plateau behind her and still not seeing him. *Where'd he go?*

When she turned back toward the plane, she was just in time to get an eyeful of Taz and Mel in their ridiculous girl-disguises, racing toward the portal of the plane. They high-fived, whooping with joy at having been rescued. Allie opened her mouth to call out to them, then snapped it shut in disbelief as they scrambled up the plane's ladder without even turning around to make sure their friends were behind them. As they disappeared inside, the rancid taste of betrayal bloomed on Allie's tongue, and the chocolate-cherry BrazilleBlast bar she'd eaten earlier threatened make a repeat appearance on her.

Allie swallowed hard, shaking her head. She'd decide later how to deal with Mel's rudeness. Right now, all that mattered was that they were saved. Her navy blue eyes found Skye's aqua ones, and she saw that Skye looked as hurt and shocked as Allie felt.

Allie had thought she'd found the perfect guy, that their relationship was just beginning, but now she wasn't sure. Maybe she was just his Alpha Island fling. Now that they were rescued and Allie was sure to get sent home, maybe Mel was already moving on. And now that he'd shown her how immature he could be, maybe Allie might be wise to move on, too. Looking at Skye, it seemed she might feel the same way about Taz.

Ever the gentleman, Darwin had turned purple with anger. "I can't believe we're related," he muttered, his hands clenched in tight fists and a frown line deeper than San Andreas creasing his forehead. He rolled his eyes and shot a look at Charlie that said "Hang on while I go get my brothers and pummel them for being such un-chivalrous morons," before sprinting toward the platinum peanut.

Charlie's the only one of us with a worthy boyfriend, Allie mused. But she didn't have time to analyze things with Mel right now. Instead, she brushed the dust off the shoulders of her flight suit and prepared to board the plane and confront whatever came next. Pasting a brave smile on her face, she tried to be happy for Charlie and not think about Mel. There would be time in the plane to sort it all out.

As Darwin disappeared inside the peanut, Allie walked over to Charlie, took her hand, and the two of them went over to get Skye. "Let's do this together," Allie whispered. The three Jackie O's would board the plane as a team. AJ, who'd been sitting cross-legged on a rock and watching the whole scene from under her sagging green tam, could board on her own.

But just as Allie's hand made contact with Skye's, she heard the plane's engine start up again. Looking at Skye's horrified expression, Allie whirled around just in time to see the ladder retracting back into the plane and the door sealing shut. Then Darwin's anguished face appeared in the driver-less cockpit, his hands pressed against the curved metallic glass and his mouth forming the words *no, no, no* just as the plane lifted into the white-hot sky.

Allie scream-sobbed along with Darwin. "No! This isn't

happening!" She felt hot tears streaming down her dusty cheeks as her hopes floated away along with the platinum peanut and the Brazille nuts housed inside.

"What is going on? How can they leave us here to fry and die?" Skye shrieked, whirling around with her hands on her hips to face Charlie and Allie as if they knew something she didn't. "This is completely illegal and totally immoral. Who sent that plane?"

Suddenly, Allie didn't even have the energy to shrug, let alone scream. It was bad enough that her boyfriend had the manners of a chimpanzee. But to be left to bake under the heat lamp of the sun like a box of stale McNuggets while the Brazille boys were on the skyway to food and water was more than she could possibly bear.

They were doomed. *Might as well accept it and start dying*.

Apparently, her body agreed. Her legs buckled beneath her as she collapsed in a dusty, miserable heap on the desert floor. She buried her face in her Purell-scented hands and closed her moist eyes, not wanting to waste any more tears since she needed the fluids. Behind her closed eyes, all she saw were angry red splotches. So this was what the end of hope looks like, she thought, her mind's eye floating above her and observing the pitiful girl curled up on the plateau floor like a crumpled-up tissue. The end of hope also had a dry throat, an empty stomach, and a broken heart. And the end of hope apparently came with a weird buzzing sound, like apocalyptic bees coming to destroy them all . . .

Buzz! Buzz!

For a minute, Allie was too busy drowning in self-pity and anticipating her own death to notice her aPod vibrating in the pocket of her flight suit. Finally, the simultaneous clicks of Skye, Charlie, and AJ's phones sliding open reached her ears.

"What now?" Allie moaned, channeling a Shakespearean monologue Careen had just assigned her in acting class. "What fresh hell is this?"

"See for yourself," muttered Charlie as she plopped on the ground next to Allie and handed over her aPod. "Un-freaking-believable."

Allie took it, expecting a texted apology from the Brazille boys, as if from the plane they would somehow have figured out how to activate the group's aPod signal again.

But what she saw was far worse than a lame, too-little-too-late hey-babe-I-totally-meant-to-go-back-and-get-you apology.

Shira's face floated on the aPod screen. Beneath her wild auburn curls, a pair of black sunglasses masked her eyes. The mogul's mouth was pursed in her usual blood-red smirk-smile. Below was a typed message.

SHIRA: MY BOYS ARE SOFT. THEY'RE NEVER GOING TO HAVE TO WORK A DAY IN

THEIR LIVES. IF YOU MAKE IT BACK, MAYBE
YOU WON'T EITHER. THERE'S NO MAP TO
LIFE. RETURN TO ALPHA ISLAND BY SUN-
DOWN TOMORROW AND PROVE YOU HAVE
WHAT IT TAKES. I'M WATCHING YOU. TRY
NOT TO DIE.

12

THE MOJAVE DESERT
TOP OF THE PLATEAU
NOVEMBER 3RD
10:30 A.M.

The propeller sounds slowly faded away as the plane floated farther into the scorched sky. Despite the heat, the stunned silence of her fellow Jackie O's, and her growling stomach, Charlie began to feel a jangly new energy seeping into her from where she stood on the desolate plateau. *Prove to me you have what it takes.* As her mind turned the text message over, it quickly became her own personal jolt of Red Bull.

Like a greyhound with a mechanical bunny, Charlie performed best when there was something to chase. And up until now, their Alphas-in-Arabia adventure didn't have that scurrying bunny to urge them forward. Sure, they'd kept going to avoid certain death. But now, it was clear Shira was perfectly aware of the Jackie O's whereabouts. This calmed Charlie's fears, since she was pretty sure Shira would never let four teenagers keel over on her watch. Shira was ruthless, but she wasn't a murderer—after all, wrongful death was a PR nightmare, and Shira was allergic to bad publicity.

Spurred by the possibility of becoming an AFL (Alpha for life), Charlie leaped up from the ground and began to look for something she could use to draw. A prickly heat rose in waves on her arms and legs. Hopefully, it was new-found motivation and not sun poisoning.

If Charlie could get the Jackie O's back to Alpha Island, maybe her resourcefulness would prove to Shira that she deserved AFL status. Charlie smiled as a second mechanical bunny popped up in her mind: Shira couldn't possibly object to an AFL being TF (together forever) with her son.

She broke a switch off a cottonwood tree growing out of a jagged clump of sandstone and began to think aloud, waving the thorny branch as she gesticulated.

"Okay. Time for plan B, or is it C? Whatever. We need to figure something out before it gets any hotter up here. So here's us," Charlie made a little star in the dust by Allie's dirt-caked foot. "And here's the island." She drew a circle a few feet away, to represent the significant distance they'd traveled.

"Super helpful, Charlie," Allie eye-rolled. "Are we going to animate ourselves back to school?"

Charlie's brown eyes met Allie's navy ones for a tense moment, but she decided to ignore her for now and concentrate on thinking up a plan. She could work on dismantling

Allie's negativity later. "Diagrams help me think," she said simply. "I wonder how many miles we are from the nearest town. If we can get a radio signal again, then maybe we can get help from one of the Death Valley towns nearby . . ."

"And we can borrow a car and drive to an airport?" Skye interjected helpfully, taking a few steps around the map and pulling her white-blond waves back into a high bun.

Charlie nod-smiled at Skye, happy that at least one of the girls was riding the wave of her thoughts to the next logical step. "Exactly. And then maybe we can charter a plane to Alpha Island."

"Who's paying?" Allie groaned. "All we have are aBucks." aBucks could be used to shop at the smoothie bar and the boutiques and spas on Alpha Island, but they were useless in the real world.

Charlie stopped pacing to wind a mahogany strand of hair around her finger. Then she remembered the string of numbers she'd committed to memory two years ago. Numbers found only on Shira's AmEx Black card. "Shira," she said emphatically, crossing her arms. "Trust me."

Perfect. A real, honest-to-Alphas plan. Charlie giggled deliriously, suddenly feeling almost manic in her excitement to get going and meet Shira's challenge head-on.

"*Trust you?* If this is such a great plan, why did it take you so long to think of it?" Allie narrowed her navy blue eyes at Charlie and shook her head. She was still sitting hunched over Charlie's aPod. "Maybe because *none of it will work*."

Charlie felt her cheeks grow even hotter than they already were. Why did Allie insist on being so negative? Did she think the best plan they had was to sit on this hilltop until buzzards pecked out their eyeballs and their status as Betas would be forever cemented? She looked down and noticed her hands were shaking.

"Okay, Al. You have the floor," Charlie said, her voice shaking with suppressed fury. "We're all ears." She was starting to feel like she might start screaming and never stop. Being stranded with Darwin was hard enough, but it was ten times worse now that he was gone. She thought back to their argument over the GPS and mentally kicked herself for being so short-tempered. At least Darwin was logical. Allie was the exact opposite of him: emotional instead of methodical, idea-negating instead of -generating.

"Why should I bother telling you what I think?" Allie piped up at last, a dejected pout blooming on her chapped lips. "You didn't want my help before. You practically laughed when I mentioned my *LOST* idea, and then it worked! You never give me any credit—"

"That is *so* not true," Charlie interrupted, her voice strangled with frustration as she began to pace the plateau. "I thought your idea to try the GPS up here was great." *But now I think you're just wasting my time*, she didn't add. Why was Allie being such a total brat?

Charlie thought back to a few weeks ago, when she'd bent over backward to make sure Allie and Mel would fall for each other, how hard she always worked to build Allie up when it came to her self-confidence. She shook her head bitterly when she thought of all those wasted hours. Because *this*—this complaining black hole of a person, the worst version of Allie—was all she got in return.

A bitter chuckle escaped Charlie's lips, her brown hair falling into her eyes as she whirled around to face Allie again. She paused for a moment and then unleashed a barb she knew would sting. "You're just mad because Mel didn't wait for you before he got on the plane."

Allie's navy blue eyes narrowed to slits, and she finally got up from her seat on the ground. "You're right, I am. How lame of me to have feelings! I should be a robot like you and make things easier on everyone."

"Guys. Enough!" Skye neatly inserted herself between Charlie and Allie, waving her arms in horizontal, air-traffic-controller motions to try to get them to take it down a notch. "Everyone's tired. And hungry. And thirsty. And *filthy*. Allie, you had a great idea, and so did Charlie. There's room in this giant kitty litter box for *both* of you to be right."

"I can't listen to this anymore," Allie cried. She whirled around and flounced off like Demi Lovato fleeing from rumors of rehab.

"Me either, actually," Charlie sighed. She took a closer

look at Skye. With her platinum hair falling out of its bun and flowing wild down her shoulders and her gold flight suit knotted at the sleeves, Skye looked like a backup dancer in an ancient Paula Abdul video. Why had she waited so long to defend Charlie against Allie's accusations? Maybe all the Jackie O's were showing their true colors. Skye hadn't contributed a thing today besides throwing herself at Taz.

"I wouldn't get involved, Skye," Charlie said. "I mean, you haven't been involved all day . . . why start now?"

Skye looked more wounded than *Saving Private Ryan* as she whirled from Charlie to Allie. "You two are being so, so . . . lame. Why all this petty fighting? I mean, aren't you supposed to be Alphas?"

"*I* am," Charlie muttered, an unfamiliar viciousness flowing through her veins. "But I'm not sure about the rest of you."

Skye's teal eyes widened, then narrowed in fury. "Wow, Charlie. Tell me how you really feel."

And then Charlie lost track of who was yelling at whom. What had started as a two-way spat quickly spiraled into a three-person hate-a-palooza. The fight was like quicksand: Once a few harsh words were uttered, it was hard not to get sucked in deep.

"Okay, you all need to take about five chamomile-melatonin supplements, STAT!" AJ might be small, but as a singer, she knew how to project. She was only five foot one, but now she towered over the three O's on a nearby boulder, the fingers of one of her tiny hands poised to pluck the spines off a saguaro cactus.

Charlie, Skye, and Allie all went quiet, gaping at AJ like she had just beamed down from outer space. The diminutive hippie had been keeping such a low profile, it was easy to forget about her.

Now that she had their attention, AJ apparently had a few things to get off her A-cup chest. "Life cannot be planned," she sighed serenely.

Charlie put a hand to her exasperated face and wished for shade, wondering how AJ didn't collapse under the heat of her green crocheted hat. Did AJ's vitamin supplements cool her from the inside?

"In this crazy universe, you can't get bogged down by rules and restrictions, by what should and should not be," AJ sermonized like she was Ashton Kutcher talking about Kabbalah. "You have to take life as it comes and challenge yourself in new ways. Which is exactly why I put veggie oil in the fuel tank."

Hold up a second, Taylor not-so-Swift.

"What?" Charlie shouted, her voice echoing. Her hands flew up to her ears, cupping them as if she couldn't possibly have heard correctly. Everything in the bright desert suddenly grew shadowy and quiet, and for a moment all she could hear was the sound of her own blood boiling.

"I said we don't know what the universe—" AJ offered lightly, oblivious to her weighty admission.

"Not *that*, you green goblin!" Allie cried, her hands in fists on her flight-suited hips and the color drained entirely from her face. "She meant the part about putting french-fry grease in our fuel tank."

"Oh, that?" AJ giggled. "I was trying to reduce our carbon emissions. It was kind of stinky but it was free of carcinogens and—"

"*Stinky?*" Skye snapped. "We all could have *died*."

"We still might!" Allie snapped.

Charlie swallowed hard, tuning everyone out. If she stayed in this conversation another minute, she might hurl. She couldn't even look at AJ right now. In fact, she couldn't look at any of them. As Allie and Skye talked over one another in a competition for who could yell at AJ louder, Charlie rode a tsunami-sized wave of anger. Her heart racing with anger, self-pity, and an urgent need to be alone. "I can't think with all of you screaming!" Surprising even herself, she whirled around on her gladiator heel and took off down the side of the mountain.

"You're leaving?" Allie called.

Charlie just nodded and kept going.

"I'm out, too!" Skye shouted.

"Same!" Allie yelled.

"You'll all thank me in twenty years when this place isn't

three degrees hotter than it is now," AJ announced.

Seconds later, their words stopped echoing. The only sounds now were distant squawks and the shuffling of Charlie's throbbing feet. She turned to sneak a peek at the plateau and discovered all three Jackie O's were gone. At least she wouldn't have to babysit anymore. Finally, she could focus on getting back to Alpha Island. It was for the best.

She pictured herself walking on the pink sand of Alpha Beach hand in hand with Darwin, telling him about this moment. Pictured herself saying *Best decision I ever made* and shaking her head at the uselessness of her former friends.

Placing a dusty hand above her forehead and scanning the empty vista below for signs of life, Charlie felt a stubborn surge of hope kicking in her chest. The sooner she got away from the dead weight dragging her down, the faster she would figure out how to fly home.

13

THE MOJAVE DESERT
THE EDGE OF DEATH
NOVEMBER 3RD
2:30 P.M.

Skye took a tiny sip from the three inches of water remaining in her A-shaped aluminum canteen, willing herself not to chug the whole thing. Once empty, there would be nothing left to fill it up. Sipping modestly, Skye could almost feel the water sloshing around in her stomach, which had been gurgling angrily for several hours now like a pissed-off friend that wouldn't stop nagging her. A lot like Allie and Charlie, actually. *You're the only company I've got out here now.* Skye sighed, patting her abs and wishing she could appease the demands of what was underneath them.

How long can people go without eating, anyway?

Skye pondered Gandhi, whose fasts lasted months. But Gandhi had shade, spectators, and a cause he believed in. The only thing motivating Skye was . . . ugh. *Why was it so hard to heat in the think? Theat in the hink? I mean, think in the heat?*

Just then, she heard a slight rustling in the brush. Training her eyes on a trembling movement amidst the scrubby desert flora, Skye stiffened. Could it be a rabbit? Maybe Skye could channel her inner Artemis and hunt her own food! Not that she could ever imagine herself eating a cute little bunny. But wearing it as a scarf after nightfall? With AJ gone, fur was finally an option.

She made a mental inventory of what she had on her—the canteen, her aPod, a cellophane wrapper from a long-finished BrazilleBlast bar, and a tube of lip gloss. Not exactly quality hunting gear. The rustling came again, and Skye began to search the ground for sticks she could use to stab the rabbit, hoping her dancer's reflexes were good enough to outrun a small mammal.

But then she caught sight of the scurrying creature. It was a useless gray desert mouse, no bigger than her thumb. *Poor skinny thing.* But maybe it would taste okay? Didn't everything weird just taste like chicken anyway? Just as Skye began calculate if the calories burned while trying to catch it would do more harm than good, it disappeared into a hole beneath a the spiny barrel of a cactus.

Skye shook her head and swallowed a moan of frustration. *No point crying over lost mice.* She knew she'd never have the guts to eat it anyway, even if she could catch it and cook it. Skye pulled out her aPod, vainly hoping for a signal she knew wasn't there. The reflection off the phone's shiny surface almost blinded her as she held it up to the sun, waving it around in a circle and praying to the cell-reception gods to give her a few bars. But the bars refused to appear.

Ugh! What good was technology if you couldn't use it when you needed it most? Skye felt hopeless tears forming in the corners of her eyes. Bar-less and scarf-less, she staggered over to a boulder and wedged herself into a tiny patch of shade beside it, telling herself she would just rest for a minute and regroup.

She still couldn't believe she'd been angry enough to try her luck alone in the wilderness. But even more surprising was the fact that Charlie had deserted them in the first place. Charlie had always been the most even-keeled and reliable of the Jackie O's. Yes, she had an intense side, but even in the extreme conditions of the desert, Charlie's behavior was totally shocking and completely out of character.

Skye sighed as she thought about it more. This game Shira had made them all play—it had changed them. They'd come to Alpha Academy to better themselves. When did it become about tearing everyone else down?

Skye thumbed the photo storage app. Instantly, a picture Taz took of himself making a face while stirring a pot of baked beans last night appeared on her screen. His ice-blue eyes were crossed and he was sticking his tongue out, but he still looked totally hawt. It became more obvious than Heidi Montag's chin implant that Taz wasn't the one for her.

All her sleepless nights, all her agonizing over how to make him see the real Skye after she'd dated his brother—all of it was for nothing. Did he really run onto the plane without her? How could he have left her like that? Everyone acted like Taz was a fearless superhero, just because he liked to fly planes and pilot boats. And nobody had invested more in the Taz brand than Skye. But just like her J. Crew ballet flats, his reputation was built on hype—guaranteed to fall apart under stress. Skye deleted the picture on her phone, feeling a nauseating pleasure in watching the image get sucked into the little Dumpster icon on her screen. She stood up and plucked a few prickly burrs from her butt. However good it felt to toss Taz out of her phone, it would feel even better to tell him off in person. She just hoped she'd get the chance.

Her head cleared after her break in the shade, Skye began walking again, this time with more determination. Her stomach growled and she started playing a game to distract herself, making a mental list of the first thing she'd like to eat when she got back to civilization. No way would she touch one of those gooey protein shakes Shira's food scientists had designed for Alpha dancers. Vomit! *No*, Skye thought as she trudged forward, her salivary glands activating at the thought of food. *What I really want is a burger. With shoestring fries. Make that a cheeseburger, extra pickles, mayo, lettuce, big, fluffy brioche bun . . .*

But just then, the smell of real food cut her burger fantasy short. Her nostrils flared, sucking up the smell like a Dyson on a mission. She stuck her sunburned nose in the air and sniffed hard. *Ohmuhgud.* It was too good to be true. Was she hallucinating? Was she already dead? Or could there actually be sausage, fresh bread, and—drool!—baked beans cooking somewhere?

Skye could have wept with joy as the smell grew stronger with each step. It was real food, she was positive. Her smile expanded and her mouth watered as she followed her nose, quickening her pace, drawn like Pavlov's dog to the delicious aroma.

Baked beans and sausage weren't exactly a dancer's diet, but she didn't care. After all, she would probably never see Mimi again.

14

THE MOJAVE DESERT
STARVATION CENTRAL
NOVEMBER 3RD
3:12 P.M.

A slight breeze had kicked up in the soundless sauna of the desert, and Allie planned to use it as a navigational tool to figure out where the delicious food smell was coming from. She licked her index finger, wincing at the bitter taste of Purell, and held it out in front of her face to see which side of her finger the air cooled. Once she knew which way was upwind, she'd be able to locate whatever was seducing her nostrils. For what seemed like forever, the smell of bread and meat had been assaulting her, leading her along the desert floor like a police bloodhound sniffing for clues to a murder. Only instead of solving a crime, Allie wanted to do the time. With a plate. And a fork. And whatever sausage-and-bun combo it was she was smelling. But all she saw in the distance was the harsh, unwelcoming desert, the ever-present sun beating down on its floor. As Allie walked, veering left whenever possible, she considered the fact of

121

Mel getting on the plane without her. The image of his butt disappearing into the cargo hold played over and over again, like a Black Eyed Peas hit on repeat in the cardio room of the 24-Hour Fitness in Santa Ana. She mulled over Mel's actions for the hundredth time that day, swallowing sausage-activated drool accumulating in her mouth.

Now that she had some time to process it, she had to admit it wasn't totally out of character for Mel to abandon her and run onto the plane. Of the whole group, he was by far the most terrified and uncomfortable in the wilderness. He belonged on a runway or in an atelier, not on a desert trail. Like a Lipizzaner stallion, those beautiful white horses bred for Spanish royalty, Mel was too pretty and too sheltered to cope in rugged conditions.

Allie shrugged her shoulders and reminded herself that whatever Mel had done, he still had a big heart. She wasn't ready to give up on him yet. Not that it would matter, since it wasn't like she'd be back at Alpha Academy anytime soon. Now that she was walking solo, the chances of her successfully hoofing it back to Shira's island were smaller than ever.

To keep her growling stomach and drooling mouth from taking over and making her lose the trail of yummy food, Allie decided to play a game of What Will I Buy. Usually, she played this game the night before heading out for a day-long mall excursion, but this time it was harder. She had to project to a point in the future after Shira's twisted contest was over and she was back in Santa Ana. She didn't want to think about Alphas clothes, even if they were state-of-the-art and made of the finest materials she'd ever worn. She saw herself in her mind's eye walking through the arches of the Santa Ana Towne Centre Mall and tried to imagine what her very first purchase would be.

But when she tried to picture her options, all the racks in her fantasy were empty. Shira's media ban meant no magazines, so Allie didn't even know what was in style—being in last season's duds wasn't part of this fantasy. Allie shook her dark blond mane, reminding herself of the one awesome thing Alpha Academy had given her. She was her own person now. She might still love to shop, but she wasn't a slave to fashion trends anymore. She would create her own style.

Maybe a cute little shift dress, she thought, designing one in her mind's eye. Maybe a retro pillbox hat. Something kind of . . . Jackie O.

Just then, Allie caught a whiff of baked beans that made her salivate Niagara Falls. The sound of voices carried to her sunburned ears, and she stopped short in front of a rock formation. Slowly, silently, she crept between two giant boulders, making sure to try to stay hidden from the view of whoever might be gathered on the other side. It sounded like five or six people, all female—would they be friendly? Should she just make herself known to them and ask for a few bites of their dinner? Maybe they were a lost desert tribe who had been forced to burn one of her J.C. Penney catalogues for warmth. Maybe they would recognize her from the eight-page back-to-school layout she did last fall and think she was some kind of goddess. Maybe they would take her in and pray to her. Pledging to fatten her up because where they come from, beauty is booty. They would teach her how to make makeup from succulents and she would amaze them with stories of love lost and found.

She just needed a way in. Something that said *I am here*, without scaring them into tranquilizer dart–throwing mode.

Allie crept along with her breath held, finally summoning up the courage to peek over the boulders. Just as she suspected, a group of girls were sitting around a flaming pit. Allie crouched low to the ground and watched as one broad-shouldered girl paced back and forth in front of a large campfire, atop which was—*ohmuhgod*. An enormous wild boar was tied to a spit, and two girls cranked it so the meat spun over their roaring fire like a horizontal gyro machine. Animal rights be dammed, a different type of pita came to mind.

Allie counted about twelve girls, all wearing the same khaki uniforms, cargo shorts with tucked-in shirts. They wore wide-brimmed straw hats with strings tied around their chins to keep them from blowing off. On their feet were hot-pink combat boots. *Did they not feel heat?*

Allie eyed their sturdy footwear enviously. While they weren't a good look, especially with shorts, they were definitely more suited to this rocky terrain than her clear gladiator sandals, which weren't doing her blisters or pedicure any favors. Allie stared down at her own outfit, a metallic silver flight suit with the sleeves and ankles rolled up—and had to acknowledge that whatever these girls were lacking in style, their clothes were far better for the terrain.

They looked like postal workers or zookeepers, but their badges were all Girl Scout.

COOKIES!

One of them—a tall, tan girl with a long braid draped over one of her broad shoulders—droned on, giving some sort of speech. Allie couldn't quite hear her monologue, but she could almost taste the crispy skin on that wild boar.

C'mon, Al. Focus. You need a plan.

She wished Charlie was here right now. Charlie could always be counted on to be logical, to plan stuff out properly and to think a plan through from all angles. Allie was impulsive and went with her heart, barging around and hoping things would magically fall into place. Whereas Charlie led with her head.

Allie sighed, still hurt and confused after losing the best friend she'd made since Trina. What happened on that plateau? How had Allie managed to drive Charlie away? *Forget it*, she admonished herself. The past was the past. All that mattered now was tearing into that pig and . . . *No! Forget Mel. Revenge is best served cold. Wild boar? Not so much.*

It was time to eat.

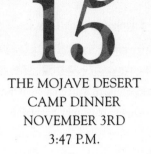

15

THE MOJAVE DESERT
CAMP DINNER
NOVEMBER 3RD
3:47 P.M.

Adrenaline coursed through Charlie's body as she prepared to dart, gazelle-like, in the direction of the roasting beast. Her peripheral vision faded to black, and all she could see from her crouched position behind a Volkswagen-sized tumbleweed was the boar roasting on the spit. Behind it, taunting her, was the cast-iron cauldron of beans.

The Scouts meeting had finally wrapped up and the pack of khaki-clad girls had filed out of their campfire circle, but Charlie was waiting until their voices sounded sufficiently far away to make her move. She didn't trust these intense nature girls to share their bounty with a dust-covered outsider in a silver flight suit, and she didn't want to have to explain to them who she was before devouring some desperately needed grub.

Maybe after she'd eaten a little, she told herself. Maybe then, she'd reevaluate and ask the girls to help her get home.

Charlie cocked her ear and frowned, still hearing faint conversation nearby even though the Scouts were out of her line of vision. Her mouth watered; she could almost taste the meat from here. Any minute now, it would be making its way into her cramping stomach. She felt a pang of remorse that Skye and Allie weren't here to reap the benefits of her find. They must be as hungry as she was, probably suffering somewhere out in the desert. Okay, and AJ, too. But if AJ were there she'd probably try and rescue the animal instead of eating it.

A Girl Scout reappeared by the roasting pit. The uniformed girl looked about the same age as Charlie. She adjusted her wide-brimmed hat before cranking the lever on the side of the spit, turning the boar so that it cooked evenly. Then the girl turned around and headed back down the same path the other Scouts had taken.

Charlie's stomach gurgled so loud that for a second she was sure the girl had heard, but there was no sign of her. She took a quick sip from her canteen and forced herself to wait a little longer. *Bide your time. Don't blow your cover.*

In order to stay patient, Charlie decided to play a game to distract herself. She imagined the first thing she would do when she arrived back at Alpha Island. *Kiss my boyfriend? Tell Shira off for putting our lives at risk? Or will I just suck it up and keep playing the game?*

Charlie truly had no idea. Lately, she'd been surprising

even herself. She knew she hadn't been easy to deal with since the plane crash, but why had it fallen to her to be responsible for everything and everyone? The Jackie O's expected her to solve everyone's problems, but nobody was stepping up to solve things for Charlie. Skye was always so caught up in the boy of the moment, and Allie was constantly entangled in some dramatic struggle with AJ or Mel. With friends like these, who needed friends? Where was the work ethic, the teamwork?

Charlie shut her eyes and replayed her outburst on the plateau that morning, wishing she'd made a passionate speech about kicking butt instead of running away from all the drama. In hindsight, she knew all the right things to say: "We didn't sacrifice everything to act like normal teenagers. We came here to win, and to win, we need to rise above this petty drama."

Buoyed by her own internal speech, Charlie opened her coffee-brown eyes and scanned the campfire area one last time. There wasn't a straw hat in sight, not a trace of Scout-chatter permeating the silent air. Surely the Scouts had drifted far away by now to prepare for dinner.

We came here to win, and I came here to eat.

Charlie was ready to make her move. She channeled her inner jackrabbit and sprang into action, leaping on pointed toes toward her delectable, delicious meal. In seconds, she had reached the campfire and stood in front of the roasting meat. She grabbed a knife that had been left in the pig's side, curling her fingers around it and pulling it out of the flesh so she could slice off a steaming, greasy bite . . .

"OW!"

Suddenly, her feet flew up beneath her and the sky and earth traded places. Charlie's head nearly scraped the dry, cracked ground as she struggled to escape the rope, swinging by her useless feet and snared tighter than a pig at a rodeo hog-tie. Her ankles were bound together above her, and she flailed upside down like a unwilling trapeze artist.

Her heart raced with terror. Her mind reeled while her body spun Cirque du Soleil circles in the air. Who were these paranoid, militaristic Girl Scouts, and how had Charlie been dumb enough to step in one of their traps?

"Um, hello? You may as well come out," she yelled, trying to keep her voice unpanicked and neutral. The last thing she was prepared to do was let them see her freak, especially if Shira was really watching.

Charlie whipped her head around and saw three sets of legs step out from behind some boulders. It was hard to get a read on their expressions from Charlie's upside-down vantage point, but one thing was for sure: Judging by their muscled legs and the professional hunter–grade trap they'd set, they were built of steel. These girls made G.I. Jane look like Kate Bosworth.

"We have another one," one of the girls barked. *Another one?* How many people had they captured? Charlie swallowed a fearful lump forming in her throat.

Charlie heard a staticky "Ten-four" come out of a walkie-talkie. She tried again to spin around on her rope to get a read on their faces, but all she could see clearly was hot-pink hiking boots, each toe box stamped with the initials WG in a bold font, with a silhouetted drawing of a tree fanning out behind the letters.

You can talk your way out of this, Charlie told herself as blood rushed to her head.

"I think there's some kind of misunderstanding," she tried. "I'm not the enemy. I'm just lost, and I stumbled onto your camp and there was nobody here and I—"

"Save it," a different set of pink shoes interrupted. "We have our orders. You can talk to Tiger Lily."

"Tiger Lily?" Charlie squeaked. "Orders?" Had she stumbled onto the set of a *Pocahontas* remake?

Suddenly, the pink shoes cut the rope that held her feet and flipped her over so she was standing up. Before she could get a look at her captors, they had pulled a dusty burlap sack over her head. *Eeek!*

Seeing nothing but brown burlap, Charlie felt two sets of hands grabbing hers. They yanked her arms behind her back and quickly tied her hands with a knot so tight it burned her wrists. A second later, flanked on either side by the demented trio of Girl Scouts, Charlie was being hustled forward along what her feet told her was the same path she'd seen these girls use earlier.

Charlie's forehead was slicked in sweat and her heart began to race even faster. She couldn't decide if it made more sense to remain quiet and agreeable or if now was a good time to start screaming. Maybe Shira would swoop in and save her, too? After all, she was kind of family, wasn't she? Two very familiar voices interrupted her thoughts. Voices that were arguing, loudly. A relieved smile spread over Charlie's face underneath the burlap sack. Too bad this Jackie O reunion had to happen in captivity.

Skye! Allie! Charlie thought-shouted, not wanting to risk giving any info to the psycho Scouts still holding her hostage. She had never been so happy to hear her two friends yelling at each other.

"Get in," one of the Scouts grunted, tugging the burlap sack off Charlie's head and shoving her into a large army-green tent.

"Ow! I'm going, no need to push," Charlie snipped, wishing more than anything that her hands weren't tied up behind her. The first thing Charlie's half-blind eyes focused on was the WG logo stitched on one wall in hot-pink thread. "Say hi to your friends."

Charlie blinked in the tent's dim light and saw Allie and Skye sitting cross-legged on the ground, their hands hogtied just as tightly as her own. "Hi." She flashed them a genuine smile, forgetting for a second how mad she'd been at her fellow O's on the plateau.

"Hi." Allie's lips twitched into a tight micro-grin, but her face was pale and her navy blue eyes clouded with fear.

"Hi. Don't bother with the knots, they're grade-A Wilderness Girl–certified." Skye sighed, her turquoise eyes flashing angrily in a shaft of dust-flecked light.

"What do they want?" Charlie whispered. Skye and Allie looked as scared as she felt.

Allie shrugged and furrowed her brow. "We just got here. They won't tell us anything. That food was a trap. Why else would they not be eating it themselves? Obvious-leh they're not counting calories."

Skye chortled bitterly, uncrossing her legs to stretch them out on the canvas-covered ground. "Obvious-leh. But the real feast is coming soon. Alpha, medium rare."

"You don't really think—" Charlie started, but her sentence trailed off.

The three Jackie O's sat in brooding, scared silence for a minute, but then one of the G.I. Janes unzipped the door and stuck her head in. "We're bringing you some grub. After you eat, you can go to the latrine for a supervised pee. Then you hang out here until we're ready to start the Tribunal."

Charlie grimaced. Sounded like a terrible few hours, but

she'd definitely eat the food. She was too hungry to care anymore. They weren't going to poison the Jackie O's now, not before the Tribunal . . .

Wait. The wha?

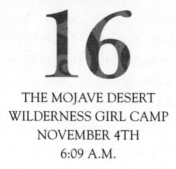

16

THE MOJAVE DESERT
WILDERNESS GIRL CAMP
NOVEMBER 4TH
6:09 A.M.

Again with the burlap sack.

This place was like a *Project Runway* challenge gone horribly wrong. Even with her hands tied tightly behind her back, Skye had managed to sleep soundly thanks to the thermal sleeping bags tossed into their tent by their jail keepers. By the time Skye opened her sleep-crusted eyes, the nature nerds had already covered her head in potato packaging.

"Ow!" Skye cringe-yelled, instantly awakened as the rough material scraped her chin, hoping she wasn't allergic to burlap. Who knew what skin contaminant lay nestled in the itchy potato-scented fibers? Facing a tribunal of potential cannibals was bad enough—she didn't want to add a bad case of chin-zits to the list.

"Is this really necessary?" Allie asked, her voice shaky and plaintive from the far corner of the tent.

If anyone answered, Skye couldn't hear.

"Let's go," her handler ordered, pulling her to her feet. Skye stumbled forward, blindly groping for the exit to the tent.

"This would be a lot easier if I could see," she pointed out as her guard directed her shoulders through the flap.

"Sorry, it's protocol," her handler whispered back. The word *sorry* was reassuring, Skye had to admit. Someone who apologized wasn't likely to chop her up into little pieces, were they?

Soon, Skye was in motion, walking to God-knew-where with nature warriors flanking her on either side to make sure she didn't bolt before the Tribunal. Whatever that was.

All she could see was the poo-brown inside of the burlap sack, but she could smell everything. There was hot chocolate (Swiss Miss Instant with marshmallows?) and frying eggs, and—*ohmuhgud*—the hissing sizzle of bacon hitting the pan. Skye stopped to get a whiff of the frying meat.

"Keep walking, astronaut."

"This is a flight suit, not a space suit," Allie snapped from somewhere nearby. "And it's Alpha Academy couture."

From the kind of school you could never get into in a million years, Skye thought.

Pretty soon, a pair of hands yanked Skye's burlap sack from her head. She blinked in the pink-and-orange light of the desert sunrise and took in her surroundings: The three

Jackie O's stood in a row under an army-green canvas shade canopy, and in front of them sat three girls, each perched on a sawed-off tree stump. Behind the stump-sitters, lined up cross-legged on the ground in two neat lines like chess pieces, sat the rest of the evil girl scout brigade, blinking their eyes at the Jackie O's and looking scarily alert, considering it was only six A.M.

Skye shivered slightly and channeled her stage training. She straightened her spine and flashed a wan smile—if only charisma could kill. There was still a chill in the desert air, but in an hour the desert would again be hotter than a habanero. She shifted her weight from one freezing foot to the other and sized up the three girls seated on the logs.

Each of the three khaki-clad girls wore her hair in an atrocious and unflattering style. Two-Braids, the apparent leader, sat in the middle, a brunette with long hippie braids trailing down each shoulder. She was short and stocky, but her hands were out of proportion to her stature and looked like they could palm a basketball. Her eyebrows were bushy and unkempt, and she had a wide, pretty mouth that would have been totally Angelina if she wasn't chomping a wad of pink bubblegum like a cow chewing its cud.

To the left of Two-Braids sat a sunburned redhead with a braid that snaked down the side and ended almost at her waist. Skye named her Side-Braid. She reminded Skye of a young Nicole Kidman, except Nicole would never wear a black bandana tied around her head like Rambo. And Side-Braid's eyelids were pink and puffy, as if she'd contracted scurvy out here in the desert, or at least a bad case of hay fever.

Finally, on the other side of Two-Braids sat Pigtails. Pigtails had dark blond hair and was slumped on her tree stump with her legs splayed. She was a little rounder than the other girls. Her gorgeous olive skin looked a shade too green, maybe because of her khaki shirt. In fact, she sort of resembled a green olive—curvy in the middle with narrow shoulders.

All three girls wore those hot-pink combat/hiking boots. In front of them was a rectangular boulder they were using as a kind of table to hold pens and clipboards.

Skye cleared her throat, wishing the Tribunal would start. A silence thicker than organic almond butter hung over the proceedings. Not one of the three girls smiled, and behind them, their uniformed minions sat there quietly like blades of khaki grass. Skye leaned forward and turned to make eye contact with Charlie, but Charlie's brown eyes were neutral and focused. She had her guard up.

Skye wished Charlie's look had been more reassuring, or at least friendly. When would Charlie get over her plateau pout?

"So," Two-Braids finally said. "Let's begin."

To Skye's left, Allie let out an incredulous snort. "Great.

Are we on *Survivor?* Where are the torches?"

Skye giggled, but the Scouts didn't seem to get the joke.

Two-Braids-One-Eyebrow stood up and began to pace in front of Allie, Skye, and Charlie.

"I don't remember there being a tribunal badge in the Girl Scouts," Charlie said icily.

Skye nodded in agreement, planting her feet in second position, her eyebrows raised in expectation.

Two-Braids shot Charlie a stern look, took a deep breath, and began to explain. "We have no affiliation with the Girl Scouts. We consider them an inferior organization. We are part of a vast worldwide community started in Norway in 1991 called Wilderness Girls. We train long and hard to survive in the harshest conditions. Our team has successfully completed wilderness challenges in Greenland, Antarctica, Peru, Mongolia, and the slopes of Kilimanjaro. We can ice-fish, scale cliff faces, spelunk into underground caves, white-water raft on class-four rapids, and survive for weeks in the wild by hunting our own food and purifying our own water. We like to show up in a wilderness area and build a campsite from natural materials, then live off the local flora and fauna."

Skye's aqua eyes rolled skyward at this speech. She was so tired of people bragging about their abilities. She got enough of that at Alpha Academy, and definitely didn't care what these Xena warrior princesses did with their time.

When was Two-Braids going to get to the part about how much they loved to hunt innocent human beings and hold them hostage?

"Thanks, profile page," Charlie snapped, saying exactly what Skye was thinking. "But considering we're being held hostage, maybe you could skip some of the details about how ah-mazing you all are and get to the point."

Two-Braids stopped pacing and turned to stare solemnly at Charlie, letting out a short sigh. "We have a moral code. This code is the foundation of everything we do." She whipped around and addressed her troops, waving her LeBron James–sized hand in the air to signal them. "Wilderness Girls!" she yelled. "What is our code?"

All thirty Wilderness Girls sat up straight and shouted the motto in unison. "TEAMWORK, TOGETHER, TODAY!"

"Must sound better in Norwegian," Allie whispered, and Skye burst out laughing for a second before managing to paste a solemn expression back on her face.

"Teamwork. Togetherness. That's what we strive for in all that we do. Without it, we would be helpless in the hands of nature. Which brings us to you." Two-Braids had a really commanding, projecting voice, Skye noticed. The other girls clearly idolized her. Weirdly, Skye felt herself growing the tiniest bit jealous of this intense, ungroomed girl and her faithful army. She had complete control out here—as long as she could build a fire and hunt, she was the best. Totally unlike the uber-sheltered life Skye had led at Alphas, and even back home in Westchester, when her every moment was ruled by the demands of school or dance. But just when Skye found she was looking forward to hearing more from Two-Braids, Side-Braid stood up, thanking her fellow wilderness wacko.

"My name is Ember, and that's Tiger Lily, who you just heard from. And over there"—she pointed a skinny, freckled arm at the olive—"is Mountain."

"Mountain?" all three Jackie O's asked.

Ember rolled her eyes. "A lot of us have hippie parents. Anyway, as Tiger explained, the WGs are committed to the principle of teamwork. We have been tracking your movements for the past twenty-four hours. Your survival rating is a two percent. Combined. Abandoning your people to face the elements alone is the exact opposite of what we believe in. We had to seize you before you infected our team with your rogue ways. "

"Understood," Charlie said, all business. "Now, will you help us get out of the desert? We kind of have to be somewhere."

Ember walked over to Tiger and Mountain. The three WGs put their heads together for a whispered conference. After a minute, Ember sat down on her stump. "What are your feelings on teamwork?"

Charlie pulled her chestnut hair behind her shoulders

and began to make their case. "We go to Alpha Academy, the school started by Shira Brazille." She paused, searching their faces for recognition. If they had heard of the Brazillionaire, they weren't letting on. "Anyway, it's very competitive but the three of us believe in teamwork more than anyone—"

"Used to, you mean," Skye blurted. Charlie had been such a team player, until yesterday on the plateau when she left her two best friends to get pecked to death by rabid buzzards.

"What?" Charlie spun around, her cappuccino-brown eyes widening at Skye.

"You used to believe in teamwork. Until yesterday. Remember? You gave up on the Jackie O's and went off by yourself."

Charlie's face flushed redder than her already-sunburned nose.

"We aren't as bad as you said we were yesterday," Allie added, her voice husky with emotion. "I know, sometimes it might seems like we're just boys and drama, but we want to win every bit as badly as you do. Right, Skye?"

"Yeah," Skye nodded. "Of course we do. But Charlie *knows* that. And she still left us there," she pointed out, as much to Allie as to the WGs, who sat watching the discussion as if it was an episode of *Hannah Montana*.

Charlie squeezed her eyes shut, took a deep breath in,

then out, like they did at the end of their Alpha Power Yoga sessions. Was she blocking out Allie and Skye, traveling to a more peaceful place? Or was she actually digesting what Skye said?

Charlie's eyes fluttered open. "I know you do. I just—I got tired. Tired of being the leader. Tired of the complaining and the negativity. But mostly I was tired of being the one that was supposed to know the answers. Because I don't. I have no idea how we're going to get back."

As Charlie talked, Skye thought back to all the drama that her friend had helped Allie get through. There was the time Allie had a crush on Darwin, or when Allie needed to find her passion or risk being expelled. And Charlie had forgiven Allie for faking her way into the Academy by posing as Allie J. way before anyone else. She had helped Allie get through weeks of being hated.

Skye had relied on Allie to help her get away from Syd, and had come rely on Charlie for masterminding tons of late-night parties and schemes. Suddenly, Skye felt a pang of guilt slice through her chest—Charlie was right. She and Allie had always come with an excess of drama. There wasn't room for Charlie's problems when those of the other Jackie O's were always so pressing.

"You're right," Allie sighed. "I showed up at Jackie O with a ton of baggage, and the AJ thing has made it so it's been all about me for way too long. But, Charlie, I swear,

I'm done. I've put AJ behind me. I'm going drama-free,"
Allie promised.

Where was AJ, anyway?

"What's done is done," Charlie said after a beat of silence.
"And anyway, I definitely gave us some unnecessary drama
yesterday. Can you guys forgive me?" Charlie's worried eyes
looked from Allie to Skye and back again. She bit her lower
lip and flashed them a shaky grin.

"Yeah," Skye said. If they didn't have each other, what
did they have? Not the boys, not a ride home. Her friends
were all she had on Earth right now. She wasn't going to
stay mad at them.

"Uh huh," Allie echoed. "Just don't freak out on us again
until we're home, okay?"

Charlie grimace-grinned. "Okay. Promise."

"Wait. Who's AJ?" Tiger asked from her stump-seat.

Allie giggled nervously. "AJ's the reason we crashed our
plane in the desert. We all split up on the plateau and I
haven't seen her since then . . ."

"There's another girl out here?" Mountain grabbed her
clipboard and a pen and started scribbling while Allie,
Skye, and Charlie spelled out the whole sordid tale, starting with the paddleboard race, then backtracking to how
Allie borrowed AJ's identity to get into the Academy, then
moving on to their not-so-brilliant plan to win the airplane
challenge.

Charlie explained the part about the boys running onto the peanut blimp.

"...and that's when we got the text message from Shira Brazille, saying we needed to get back to Alpha Island in twenty-four hours. *Or else.*" Charlie's eyebrows shot skyward as she shot the WGs a look that implied what *or else* might mean.

"Interesting challenge," Tiger said, her chin resting in her sizable hand.

"We'll help you," Ember said quickly. "Right, WGs?"

The other two Tribunal judges nodded. Mountain spoke next, reading from her clipboard. "You've proven you're capable of amazing levels of teamwork, in spite of going to school in an environment that promotes individuality, competition, and ruthlessness. But before we help you, we need to find AJ."

"Do we have to?" Allie asked.

Tiger shot her a stern look. "You can't leave a girl behind. It goes against everything the WGs stand for."

"Of course," Charlie hurriedly agreed. "We would never leave her here."

"Hang on," Skye spoke up, suspicion clouding her clear blue eyes. Nobody was asking the most important question of all. Charlie and Allie might be eager to get home, but why should they trust these girls, who a few minutes ago had the Jackie O's scared out of their minds? "Why would you help us? I mean, what's in it for you?"

145

After a beat of contemplative silence, Tiger answered. "Because that's what WGs do. It's part of our code. And besides," she added, a half-smile forming on her almost-Angelina lips as her brown-black eyes looked Skye, Charlie, and Allie over with interest, "there is something you can do for us."

"Can we eat something first?" Allie asked.

"That's probably best," Tiger said. "You're going to need all the energy you can get." She exchanged a look with the other girls and giggled. There was something in their laugh—like an extra dash of sugar—that made Skye uneasy. Like meat that had been over-seasoned to cover up a bad taste. Not that she cared. At this point, meat was meat, no matter what it tasted like or how much it cost.

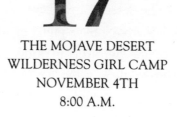

17

THE MOJAVE DESERT
WILDERNESS GIRL CAMP
NOVEMBER 4TH
8:00 A.M.

"Let me get this straight," Allie said, rubbing her full belly. "*You* guys want a *makeover?*"

"Not all of us," Mountain surveyed the crowd of WGs before turning back to face Allie, all the while tugging anxiously on her pigtails. "We just want a few examples. Once you do a couple of us, we can show the others. We're fast learners."

Tiger and Ember nodded in agreement, eyeing the three Alphas nervously. All of a sudden, Allie realized, the hiking boot was on the other foot. Now the Alphas held the cards, and the WGs were the frightened ones. Just thinking about it, Allie instantly relaxed. Because if there was anything she was the undeniable expert on in this crowd, it was beautification.

"There must be more at stake here than a fashion statement," Charlie's curious brown eyes darted over the three head WGs, searching for clues. "Why would you need make-overs out here in the desert?"

"It's obvious-leh a boy," Skye piped up, grinning knowingly while stretching her arms in wide circles now that Mountain had untied them.

When Tiger blushed, Allie knew Skye had guessed her secret.

"Okay, fine. It's a boy," Tiger boomed, her commanding presence still impressive to Allie. Even while awkwardly revealing embarrassing personal details, Tiger's confident, all-natural demeanor was impressive.

"May as well explain," Ember chided, placing her freckled hand on Tiger's back to prompt her to elaborate.

Tiger sigh-groaned, her eyes flitting over the Jackie O's as if trying to gauge whether or not she could trust them. "Okay," she said at last. "My best friend—besides the WGs, of course—is this guy named Wyatt Yellowstone. He's the head of the strongest pack of Eagle Scouts in the Southwest. He's so . . . capable."

"And gorgeous!" Ember interjected.

Tiger shrugged her off, continuing. "And I can match him in any outdoor activity, so he's always been impressed with me. But lately, it seems like stir-frying beetles isn't enough."

Ew!

"Enough for what?" Allie interrupted, gagging a little at the image of fried beetles.

"Enough to keep his attention on me. Which is where I want it," Tiger admitted, blushing a deep purple under her tan.

"You mentioned earlier that you turned your boyfriends into girls for the PAP race," Mountain reminded them, flipping the pages of her clipboard to review her notes. "So we WGs must have a shot at looking more . . . girly." Mountain smiled at Allie, her brown eyes twinkling with hope.

Allie side glanced at Skye. *Good luck with that!*

Skye side glanced back. *And then some.*

Charlie shot them both a look. *They're hairy but they're not stupid. Stop being so obvious!*

"We know it seems weird," Ember conceded. "We believe a girl should be able to survive out in the wild, to build her own shelter and kill her own food. We've always believed that. But we're starting to feel like our skills in the area of boys are . . . insufficient. Shouldn't a girl be able to track a prairie dog, wrestle it, kill it, cook it, eat it, *and* have a boy want to hold her hand at the campfire? Can't we have it all?"

"I get it," Allie said, nodding furiously. "You want to start the fire and light a fire. I'm with ya."

"Um, right." Mountain nodded like she knew what Allie was implying, even though she probably didn't. "So, will you help us?"

"Of course," Skye answered, pulling a loose wavelet of

her platinum hair back into her bun. "We'll scratch your back, and then you scratch ours. Can you get us home by sundown? That's our absolute deadline."

Mountain, Tiger, and Ember leaned in for another whispered conference. Ember nodded, then pulled away from her fellow tribunal judges. "We'll do everything we can to get you home in time. We have resources and manpower—er, womanpower. Once we find your friend AJ, we'll do everything we can to get you home."

"Good," Charlie nodded. "Then we have a deal. There's one semi-major problem with this scenario, though."

Skye nodded. "We don't have the right equipment."

"Equipment? Like what? We have a Norwegian Wilderness Knife with over three hundred mini pop-out tools." Ember gave Skye a blank look.

Allie giggled. These girls really were clueless about beauty. But luckily for them, they'd captured her, Allie A. Abbott; she may not know how to pitch a tent or find water in the center of a cactus, but she knew the elements of style and beauty like she was born in a salon.

This was her biggest beauty challenge to date, though. How would she take three girls who'd never used a blowdryer, and all without even the most rudimentary tools of the trade? Too bad there wasn't a TV crew to document the transformation. Something like this would pull big ratings.

"Tools are the least of it," Skye informed the WGs. She

began listing what they would need in order to make the Wilderness Girls into glamazons. "We need makeup. And hot wax. Deep conditioner. A sewing machine for your clothes, or better yet, new clothes. That's just for starters." As she listed out her requirements, Skye's voice sounded more and more doubtful they could pull it off.

And as Skye talked, the three WGs postures went from erect to abject. They slumped onto their tree stumps in defeat, their enthusiasm for Project Wilderness Makeover growing fainter by the second.

Allie wracked her brain, flipping the pages of her internal grooming encyclopedia. Suddenly, she had it: a vision for each girl, and a plan to make it all happen.

Allie drew herself up to her full height, feeling confident in front of the intimidating WGs for the first time. "Hang on, Skye. I've got this." Allie cleared her throat and raised her voice so the entire Wilderness Army could hear her. "I can make you all look your best, but only if you promise me you'll always remember there's more to life than looking hot."

Allie's navy blue eyes scanned the crowd, as each of the seated WGs nodded in agreement. Satisfied, she turned to Mountain and motioned to her to get her pen ready to write.

"Great. Mountain, for you, we'll do a Natalie-Portman-meets-Lea-Michele look. Natural, fresh, but with an edge. Tiger, you're a great fit for Angelina Jolie from her Lara

Croft period. You've got her lips and her toughness. And Ember, you're obvious-leh destined to look like pre-Botox Nicole Kidman, like maybe from *Days of Thunder*. But with the freshness of Lindsay Lohan from *Mean Girls*. You're all going to look ah-mazing!" Allie clapped her hands together gleefully, channeling Tyra Banks during makeover week on *ANTM*.

"But, Al. All we have to work with is, like, our own spit and some dish soap," Skye pointed out.

Allie shook her head, a wide grin spreading across her lips. "We're going to make our own products. Here's what we'll need: eucalyptus leaves, bottled water, desert sand, cactus extract, the bone ribs from a small desert carcass, mud from under a boulder, preferably one infused with peat moss, and the saliva from a Western banded gecko."

Mountain scribbled furiously, nodding as she wrote, like it wouldn't be a problem to find any of it.

Charlie and Skye burst out laughing, amazed at what Allie had come up with.

"Where did all *that* come from?" Charlie asked between giggles.

"What?" Allie giggle-shrugged. "Am I the only one of us who reads *Organic Style*?"

"You've been holding out on us!" Skye chortled, wiping a laugh-tear from beneath her eye.

Allie laughed, too, reveling in the feeling of having her

besties back. The only thing worse than going it alone in the desert was thinking her friends had given up on her. Now that the three O's were reunited and on good terms, they'd hit this makeover out of the Mojave and show Shira they all deserved to be Alphas for life.

18

"GO, GO, GO!" Tiger Lily's screaming voice floated back down the churning water to Charlie's ears as she jumped from one river rock to the next, struggling to keep up with the remade Wilderness Girl. Tiger's chestnut-brown hair was now soft and shiny, trailing down her back in a waterfall of waves instead of dowdy braids, but Tiger Lily was still totally hardcore, leaping among river rocks like she was starring in a human version of *Frogger*. Charlie had already come close to getting swept away by the rapids at least three times, but Tiger never faltered. Her feet Spiderman-ed to the rocks.

Tiger Lily had led the tracking expedition to this river by following AJ's scent (for once, Charlie was glad she wore so much patchouli). The WGs were so psyched about their makeovers that they'd offered to show the Alphas a few more wilderness skills while they tried to pick up the scent again. They'd been doing white-water drills for nearly

154

an hour, and Charlie was exhausted but also invigorated. Before today, she would have assumed she had zero in common with a girl like Tiger, but they'd actually become fast friends.

Charlie squinted upriver, where Tiger waved at her from a huge boulder. She gulped a sip of water from her canteen and began to navigate the rocks again. Waves crashed against the stones as Charlie panicked, then jumped, then panicked again, then jumped again. Getting closer to Tiger's spot in the center of the river, Charlie couldn't help noticing how radiant the chief WG looked. Her skin glowed thanks to Allie's desert-sand-and-aloe exfoliator, and her newly plucked eyebrows showed off her gorgeous bone structure.

"I gotta say it again, Tiger. You look amazing." Charlie smiled as she made the final leap onto Tiger's boulder and joined her new friend. "Thanks for showing us all these wilderness skills."

"No problem," Tiger grinned, revealing a single dimple in her left cheek. Shyly, she looked at the ground. "Thanks for prettifying me. I can't wait to get home and surprise Wyatt at the next Wilderness cookout. Hopefully, all those beauty tricks you guys taught me will stick."

The truth was, Tiger had taught Charlie a million more important things than the few beauty tips the Alphas passed along. They'd covered which leaves not to brush up against in the wild, how to pee standing up (holding on to a tree trunk helped), how to combat B.O. without deodorant, how to train their eyes to see in the dark, how to extract water from cacti, how to kill a nest of fire ants . . . the list was endless. Now Tiger was focused on teaching them to be quick on their feet, to work with nature rather than fight against it.

Charlie smiled as she caught sight of Mountain and Allie leaping over the trail of river rocks to join them. "Go, Allie!" she yelled, her heart surging from the drama of the river race and the joy of having her besties back.

"We made it!" Allie yelled on her final jump, staggering atop the island and running over to give Charlie a sweaty hug. "This is actually fun!"

Charlie nodded vigorously in agreement.

"Okay," Tiger said, putting on her game face once Mountain and Allie had each taken a swig from their canteens. "New drill. Here's the scenario: You've dropped your pack into the rapids and have no provisions or tools. Now you're being chased by a ferocious desert rat. Strong possibility it has rabies. What do you do, soldiers?!"

Allie went into *Avatar* mode and channeled her best Na'vi. Her face hardened, and she suddenly looked more amphibious than a tree frog. "Cover myself in river mud and lie low!" she cried.

Tiger raised one of her ping-pong paddle–sized hands and gave Allie a loud high five. "Right on, soldier."

Just then, Ember and Skye appeared on the riverbank twenty feet away, waving their hands wildly and shouting at the girls on the rock island to come out of the river and meet them.

"They must have found the scent," Tiger said. She reached into her pack and pulled out a hot-pink rope, threw it over a low-hanging tree branch, and quickly fashioned a pulley system using a carabiner. She motioned for the Alphas to hop on.

Allie went first, her hands gripping the metal carabiner so hard her knuckles turned white. She screamed as she slid along the rope to the riverbank, but flashed Charlie and the WGs two thumbs up from shore.

Charlie followed Allie, holding her breath as she whizzed along over the rapids, then gasping for air once her feet made contact with the muddy bank.

Once everyone made it across, Ember explained. "We picked up the scent of AJ's tea tree oil back there," she said hurriedly, gesturing behind her to a thicket of sage bushes and cacti. "I think she's headed north."

"We'd better hurry," Tiger nodded. The group set out along the river's edge, Charlie and Allie bringing up the rear with Skye and Ember leading the way. Charlie tried to ignore the uneasy churning of her stomach. Surely with these expert trackers, they would find AJ and get back to Alpha Island before Shira's deadline. It had to work out, she told herself. They'd earned a little luck, hadn't they?

"Ohmuhgud," Charlie heard Skye say as they reached the top of a small hill lined with craggy rocks. "That's AJ's."

Charlie hurried to the top of the hill, scared to look but unable not to.

Uh oh. Charlie stared at the green object flapping in the wind, dangling high up on a branch like a discarded parachute. It was definitely AJ's grubby green tam.

Her terrified brown eyes found Allie's navy blue ones. Allie looked just as scared as Charlie felt. Charlie spun around in the futile hope that AJ was hiding somewhere nearby, enjoying watching them get punked. But she was nowhere in sight.

Charlie felt downright ill. If AJ was injured—or worse than injured!—because of Charlie's plateau freak-out, she would never forgive herself. AJ might have been senseless enough to cause their PAP crash, but she didn't deserve a violent end. She was green, but she wasn't *evil*.

But just as Charlie began to create a dozen guilt-induced scenarios of what might have befallen the teeny greenie—coyote attack, killer bees, axe murderer, the list was endless—a simultaneous *ping* rang out from all three Alphas' pockets.

That *ping* meant one thing, and one thing only. Their aPods had reception!

Charlie patted herself down like an airport TSA agent, frantically searching for her phone. It had been so long since she'd needed it that she couldn't remember which pocket it was in. At last, she found it in a zippered cargo pouch against her right thigh. Her hands shook as she scrolled through her text messages, praying there wouldn't be something about AJ showing up dead.

First, she had to wade through a few dozen texts from a very apologetic Darwin.

Darwin: Can't believe the plane door shut! Feel terrible! Sending help ASAP.

Darwin: Please tell me you guys are okay. Taz and Mel are morons.

Darwin: Charlie? I'm so sorry. Can't reach my mom. Trying for an outside signal to call the National Guard.

Darwin: Please tell me you're out there.

Charlie paused mid-text, looking up at Skye and Allie. "You guys must have like a hundred texts from Mel and Taz, apologizing for the plane thing."

Allie sighed. "You'd think, but nope."

"Me either," Skye said, her aqua eyes rolling. "Do they even get how rude they were?"

"Guess not," Allie murmured, looking back at her phone.

Charlie's stomach clenched into an anxious fist. She looked down at her phone, thumbing past the million messages from Darwin, expecting the worst. She could feel the gorp she'd eaten earlier with Tiger threatening to come back up.

At last, Charlie found the text from AJ at the bottom of her inbox. *Phew, at least she's alive!*

But Charlie's relief morphed instantaneously into panic when she read AJ's message. She heard Skye murmur *Uh oh*, which meant AJ had made sure to write to all the Jackie O's.

AJ: See you around, Betas! I'm about to make it back first. There can only be one Alpha. And there's no U in one.

Needles of disappointment and frustration pricked Charlie's skin, but inside she felt numb. So numb, she might as well have been dead. But also, weirdly, underneath it all, she felt relief. She closed her eyes and pictured the river she had just jumped through. Like getting washed away in the swirling rapids, there was a perverse comfort in the idea that even if she didn't win Shira's twisted competition, the struggle would finally be over.

So this is what it's like to lose.

Charlie shrugged her shoulders, as if trying the outfit of "loser" on for size. Maybe she could make her peace with what AJ had done and move on with her life. That would be the easiest thing to do.

But then a wave of anger mixed with bitter frustration flowed through her veins. She closed her eyes and balled up her filthy, mud-crusted hands balling into furious fists and pounding her forehead. "That's it," she sigh-moaned sarcastically. "Game over. Winner take all, losers go home."

When Charlie opened her eyes, she saw Allie shaking her head, hard. So hard her dark blond river-soaked hair flew around her face. "No. No, no, no. We are not losing to AJ. This isn't over."

"All that work," Skye said glumly, ignoring Allie's denial. Her foot arced gracefully in front of her before making contact with a tree root sticking out of the mud and kicking it repeatedly. "And AJ, the least Alpha of Alphas, outsmarts us in the end. Obvious-leh the veggie oil in the plane was all part of her sabotage."

The WGs looked appalled.

Charlie looked at the horrified expressions on the faces of Ember, Mountain, and Tiger. Her eyes misted over. She couldn't help it—in spite of all her newly acquired wilderness warrior skills, she hadn't learned how to keep angry tears inside where they belonged. She sat down on a dead log and snuffled, cringing inside but unable to stop. *Pathetic!*

Tiger sat down next to her and put a tan, sinewy arm around Charlie's shaking shoulders. "Stop crying, Charlie," she said. Her voice was quiet yet firm.

"Why?" Charlie managed, choking on an embarrassing sob-snort. "What does it matter?"

"It matters. You need to look good for your homecoming. Honorary Wilderness Girls aren't teary-eyed."

Homecoming?

Ember nodded, pulling a small army-green walkie-talkie from her pack. "We'll beat AJ back. No way we're letting her get there first after she crashed your plane. That's just *wrong.*"

"What about teamwork?" Skye asked. "I thought we had to find her before we left."

"There's no AJ in teamwork!" Tiger jumped up off the log and pulled Charlie up with her. "Ember, the walkie."

Ember nodded, flipping a switch. The radio buzzed to life in her freckle-dotted hands, and she passed it over to Tiger.

A wide, Angelina-esque smile filled Tiger's glowing face as she spoke into the walkie-talkie. "Lone Ranger to Scout Mobile. Come in, Scout Mobile. Ready for immediate pickup. CODE MAMA GRIZZLY. I REPEAT, CODE MAMA GRIZZLY."

Huh? Charlie stared open-mouthed at Tiger Lily's perfect hair framing her polished face, too dejected to even ask what she was up to. But within minutes she heard the blades of a helicopter slicing noisily through the sky, and a few seconds later, a silver copter dipped into view, swooping lower until it hovered a hundred feet above them.

Charlie's heart soared. Had Darwin finally gotten the National Guard to find them? She grinned at Allie and Skye, flashing a thumbs-up in the din of the helicopter propeller. Both girls smiled back, then pointed at Tiger and gave another thumbs-up.

Charlie looked back up at the copter and realized this wasn't the National Guard *or* an Alpha Plane. Emblazoned on the side of aircraft, etched into the silver, was the same WG-plus-tree logo the scouts had on their boots. Charlie made a mental note to someday find a way to repay Tiger. For now, she ran up to the tall wilderness warrior and squeezed her in a tight hug.

A hatch popped open in the bottom of the plane and a pair of hands dropped a rope-ladder down until it dangled just above Tiger Lily. "Hop aboard," she yelled.

Charlie allowed herself a sliver of hope as she grabbed the ladder and scrambled up toward the helicopter. If they put the heli-pedal to the metal, maybe they could actually pull off an upset and beat AJ back to Alpha Academy.

It's not over till the skinny singer screams, she thought, placing one foot above the other as she hustled up the wobbly rope ladder. With any luck, her next visit to Alpha Island would be just like this moment: a speedy climb to the top.

19

The sun glowed red in the dimming sky as the WGs' emergency helicopter zipped toward Alpha Island like a giant hummingbird. Inside the copter, Skye smoothed her hands over her new outfit, wishing the Wilderness Girl uniforms had a bit more pizzazz but happy to finally be out of her grubby Alphas flight suit. Once they had all hoisted themselves into the copter, Tiger had handed Skye, Allie, and Charlie each a stack of starched, crisply folded khaki shirts and shorts. Even if the uniforms were closer to UPS than AFL, the clothes were perfect for jumping and beating AJ to the finish line.

Skye's teal eyes shot sideways at Charlie and Allie sitting next to her, and she saw that they looked as excited and nervous as she felt. Charlie was making some sort of Charlie-ish list on her aPod, while Allie was busy rubbing Purell between her sandaled toes. They were readying themselves for whatever awaited them back at Alpha Island—the good, the bad, and the angry.

For the first time since the plane crash, Skye felt the stirrings of real optimism thrumming in her chest. She wished she could embrace the positivity and execute a few pirouettes, but she was strapped to a metal bench against the wall of the helicopter cabin. The best she could do was twirl her ankles and crack her wrists to the rhythm of a whirring propeller, while mentally leap-spinning through space. She took a swig of river water from her canteen and directed her feet from first to second to third position on the aircraft's floor. She peeked into the cockpit, where the pilot, a girl the WGs called Sarge, was gunning the engine, her ears obscured by giant plastic earphones and her eyes covered in tinted goggles. When Tiger had explained the situation—that they were racing to beat another aircraft back to Alpha Island—Sarge had nodded, remarking that she'd never lost an air race in her life.

Skye sat back and reviewed the past forty-eight hours, knowing that the minute they landed she'd have no time to think, only to act. Images from the PAP crash flashed through her mind, followed by the fun night with the boys around the campfire, her kiss with Taz, the scary night they'd spent in the WGs' tent, and the friendships they'd ended up making. When a memory of the awful fight on the plateau surfaced, Skye shook her head and tossed it away. All that was behind them now.

Training her eyes on Charlie and Allie sitting beside her, Skye lifted her chapped lips in a bemused smile. While the past few days had held some of the lowest lows she'd ever experienced, their time in the Mojave had also been surprisingly fun.

She sighed with relief over the biggest accomplishment of all—making up with Charlie and Allie after the plateau blowout. She couldn't imagine the game ending with the three Jackie O's not on speaking terms. Now that they'd made it through this, she knew Charlie and Allie were the real deal—the kind of besties she would keep as FFLs (Friends For Life). If a plane crash, a wilderness expedition, nearly dying of thirst, and getting held hostage in a tent didn't bond you to your friends, what would?

Sarge's voice crackled over the helicopter speakers. "Stand by for landing."

Across the cabin, the three WGs sat on the bench opposite Skye's. Ember gave her a thumbs-up and Skye mimicked the gesture, flashing a toothy smile at her new friend. Then she turned and stared out the window at the @-shaped island rising out of the woman-made ocean below, its curved tail sparkling with pink phosphorescent sand.

She shivered at a sudden realization: The next time she

saw this view, she would be flying home—either expelled or as an Alpha for life.

Skye began to search the island, her eyes combing the campus for signs of life as the copter lowered its altitude. Where was everyone? The campus seemed deserted. No metallic-clad girls lounged outside on the great A-shaped lawn. Nobody hurried to class at the Sophocles Theater Arts Building or the Marie Curie Inventor's Lab or—and here Skye shuddered, realizing that an empty campus meant a lot of people she loved had probably been expelled—to the dance cube that dangled sixty feet in the air above the island. Had all her fellow bun-heads been kicked out?

Eyes on the prize, she reminded herself. There was no point in worrying about the fates of her dance buddies Ophelia, Tweety, and Prue right now. It would only slow her down. Besides, if she won, it would be a win for them, too. Skye nodded decisively, her platinum wavelets bouncing a little. If she was crowned AFL, she would find a way to help the bun-heads in their own careers.

Because it's all about teamwork. A little laugh escaped Skye's lips. The WGs had rubbed off on her more than they knew.

The second the helicopter touched down on the great lawn, Tiger jumped up and began unbuckling the Alphas from their safety harnesses. "Move, move, move!" she yelled, in full WG platoon-leader mode. "This is a race, remember? Every second counts."

Skye remembered. She threw off her harness and bolted from the bench, Charlie in front of her and Allie behind. Seconds later, the three Jackie O's jumped the ten feet from the copter door and onto Shira's sweater-soft blue-green lawn, made of a special variety of grass flown in from New Zealand. *I'll miss this island* was Skye's first thought as she rolled onto the sweet-smelling grass. Her second thought was more upbeat: *Maybe someday I'll buy this island.*

"No time for goodbyes," Tiger grunted, jump-rolling onto the grass along with Ember and Mountain.

"Thanks for everything," Charlie said, her eyes a little teary. "We had the time of our lives with you."

Skye felt a lump forming in her throat. The WGs were awesome; she didn't want to say goodbye. She grabbed Ember, who'd guided her through the river and taught her how to repel down a cliff, and placed her hands on either side of her freckled, made-over face. "Bye, Ember. You're totally ah-mazing. Thank you for everything!" she cried, her voice thick with emotion.

"We'll look you up as soon as this is over," Charlie assured the three WGs as they practically shoved her toward the Pavilion. "See you in the real world—"

"Enough," Mountain yell-smiled. "Go! Win this thing." She winked and waved them forward.

So the Jackie O's began to run. And all Skye could hear was the pounding of three sets of WG-imprinted pink combat boots on the gravel. The flowery smell of the island's wild plumeria engulfed her and giant ferns thwacked at her shoulders and her furiously pumping arms as she sprinted toward to the Pavilion. Up ahead, the bris-soleil shades began to open up on the tall metallic building like the wings of a phoenix, as if welcoming them home.

Which meant someone was inside.

The pounding of Skye's footfalls was so rhythmic, so loud, that it seemed to almost be a chant, as if her feet were ordering her to keep going. *Win this thing. Win this thing. Win. This. Thing.*

Sprinting alongside Charlie and Allie, Skye knew one thing for sure: She wanted this more than anything else in the world. And maybe wanting something badly enough was worth something.

Skye's mind raced as her lungs burned from exertion. AJ couldn't possibly want this as much as Skye did. The girl had already gone platinum as a singer. Twice. And besides, AJ had sabotaged them. She refused to believe that dirty tricks could lead to a win. Not when the stakes were this high. Skye's internal chant grew more focused as her breathing became more labored. *Beat AJ! Beat AJ! Beat AJ!*

Suddenly, the round doors of the Pavilion—bordered on both sides with fluorescent orange and pink flowers in ALPHAS-shaped beds—were twenty, then ten, then five feet away. A foot ahead of them now, Charlie turned around and flashed Skye and Allie a wild-eyed grin.

They were close enough to taste victory.

"I want all three of us to win this," Charlie panted. "We need to arrive as a singular unit."

Charlie's hands shot outward. Skye took one and Allie took the other. Skye's heart began a Janelle Monáe tap-inspired dance sequence in her chest. She took a gasping breath, exhaling as the three O's barreled through the doors together, their smiles wide enough to show the world every one of their Whitestrip-enhanced teeth.

Together, they were the embodiment of teamwork, of triumph, of *Alpha*.

Bursting through the doors of the theater, Skye's high-wattage smile fizzled to a power-outage pout. The perfectly circular room was empty and dark. Except for one person sitting calmly in the center of the round stage under the glare of a single spotlight.

It wasn't AJ waiting for them.

It was Shira.

The bossy Aussie's blood-red lips formed a tight smile, one perfectly plucked eyebrow raised above her trademark black sunglasses in silent greeting. Her Pilates-toned butt perched atop a hoverdisc, and she sat with her legs primly crossed, her patent-leather Prada pumps dangling just a few inches above the floor.

Skye's heart sank as she skidded to a halt at the top of the stairs. Shira had returned to Alpha Island to end this crazy competition once and for all. But the dark, lonely theater told Skye everything she needed to know—they were too late, and they had lost the race. AJ had beaten them back after all, and now it was execution time.

Skye blinked back angry tears as her eyes searched the empty bleachers in vain for a muse rolling her monogrammed suitcase.

Charlie's hand squeezed hers, but it wasn't enough to quell Skye's disappointment. Nothing would be. Not for a long time. In fact, not ever.

"G'day, lollies," Shira purred, breaking the horrible silence of the theater. She hopped off her hoverdisc and planted her stilettos on the shiny white stage, placing her pale hands on either side of her slender waist. She wore a long black dress that shone in the spotlight like wet asphalt.

"Hello," Charlie squeaked.

"Hello," Allie whispered.

"Hi," Skye managed. Her mouth was dryer than the desert she'd just flown out of.

"Did you have a nice flight?" Shira asked, as though making small talk over tea.

Three sets of khaki-shirted shoulders shrugged nervously in response.

Let's get this over with. Skye straightened her posture, sticking out her B-cups in preparation for her execution.

"Never mind. Let's get to it, shall we? Over the past few weeks, each of you had tried your very best to distinguish yourself as a leader. But the truth is, there can only be one true Alpha."

Spit it out!

"And it isn't AJ."

Skye's mouth fell open into a shocked oval.

Not AJ? Then who?

She choked back a sigh that teetered on a sob, wishing Shira would just get to the point.

Out of the corner of her eye, Skye thought she saw something flickering in the darkened rows of empty audience seats behind Shira. She blinked hard and looked again, but the flicker was gone.

Maybe she had sun poisoning from her desert adventure after all. Not that it mattered now, at the end of the game. She'd have plenty of time to recuperate back in Westchester.

"*You.* The one and only Alpha is *you*," Charlie whispered, her brown eyes drilling angry holes in Shira's head. Skye's breath caught in her throat. *Of course.* A single tear fell down Charlie's pink cheek, as if punctuating the end of her sentence. "And this was all for nothing."

"Chah-lie, you were always so smart," Shira smile-hissed. "But you're only half right. The only Alpha left on this island is me."

"But this wasn't all for nothing," Allie mused, trying to figure out the puzzle, since the Aussie wasn't talking. "Because we learned to *follow our passions* and *believe in ourselves?*" Allie's voice dripped with tired clichés and sarcasm as she anticipated the lame speech that was sure to come next.

Skye stared at Shira, waiting for an answer she didn't want to hear, wishing she'd never set foot on Alpha Island. Because if this whole competition, with all its broken hearts, was truly just one more of Shira's manipulative games, then Charlie was right. It had all been for nothing.

Skye thought of the ballet slipper her mother had given her, the one that was supposed to make all her hopes and dreams come true. She shook her head bitterly and stared at the shiny white floor beneath her feet. The HAD slipper hadn't worked. It was just a pointe shoe without a point.

"All correct, Allie. You did learn to follow your passions and believe in yourselves. And you learned how to get around the rules of my island," Shira added. "Which is why you'll be leaving it soon. *Forever.*"

So much for hopes and dreams; this was the stuff of nightmares.

20

Allie felt her hands clench into angry fists, her fingernails digging half-moon indentations into her palms as she stood at the top of the dimly lit steps.

She was trying to absorb Shira's words, but something refused to click.

What she understood: They had lost. They were being sent home. The Jackie O's were not invincible, and there was no winner in Shira's insane competition. She understood the *what*, but not the *why*. She blinked her navy blue eyes and ran a hand absently through her desert-dusted hair, struggling to fit the puzzle pieces together.

Why would a billionaire like Shira Brazille build an entire island, an entire *biosphere*, devoted to a school for exceptional girls, then send them all home with nothing? It made no sense. It was like if Victoria's Secret suddenly

176

had a buy-one-get-one-free bra sale without even bothering to promote their new fragrance line. *Shira's actions were bad business*. And if there was one thing Shira Brazille fiercely guarded, it was Brazille Industries. Her business sense was famously flawless. That was why she'd started Alpha Academy in the first place—to pass on her secrets of success. Or that's what she had made them all believe. Allie looked down at her WG-issued hot-pink combat boots and wondered what—if anything—Shira had told them that was actually true.

Just as she was about to stammer out this final question to Scary Shira, Allie looked up to see a twinkling, shimmering holographic curtain rising behind the stage.

Allie gasped, her face burning with the shock of what she saw. The hundreds of seats had only appeared empty. In fact, the auditorium was packed! Yet another lie to add to the list, Allie noted. But she was too distracted by the scene before her. People, seated in row upon row of the audience. Each one of them was applauding. The roar of a thousand clapping hands nearly knocked her over.

Ohmuhgud.

Allie screamed when she spotted her mom and dad in the second row. Her skinny, Jazzercise-addicted mom waved wildly at Allie and blotted her tear-stained cheeks with a wad of tissues. Next to her mom, her red-faced dad put his arms over his balding head and yelled, "That's our girl!" Allie did a double take, her vision swimming with shock. The last—and only—time Allie had seen her dad's eyes misting over like this was when the Red Sox won the World Series.

Seeing her parents crying tears of pride, everything fell into place. Allie waved at them, a delirious and slightly teary smile replacing her original look of shock.

Because now Allie had solved the puzzle. She knew the *why*.

Shira was a genius, and the Jackie O's were famous.

"What. The. Hell. Is. Happening," Charlie whisper-screamed over the roar of the crowd, her hand finding Allie's and squeezing as if she was juicing a lemon.

Skye looked puzzled, too, scanning the crowd nervously, her mouth twitching with a confused half-smile.

Allie nodded, not surprised she'd been the first Jackie O to figure it out. Because she may not know how to dance a flawless rendition of *Swan Lake*, or how to hack computers, but Allie knew a reality-TV finale when she saw it.

And this moment, this was clearly their last episode.

"The whole thing was a hoax," she whisper-shouted to Charlie and Skye over the thunderous applause, careful to smile big for the hidden cameras she was now sure were trained on their faces. "It's a TV show!"

"Huh?" Charlie and Skye said in unison, their heads whipping around to look at Allie.

Allie leaned over and grabbed Skye's hand so they were standing in a circle. She didn't have much time. "Listen, you'll understand in a second, when they do the big reveal. But now, just smile as big as you can and be your beautiful selves. As God is my witness, we are going to come out of this looking *ah-mazing*. Or my name isn't Allie A. Abbott! Just remember, smile and walk, smile and walk. Our fans are waiting."

And with a steely resolve, like a Miss America contestant making a tiaraed victory lap, Allie licked her lips so they shone and produced her most dazzling smile ever.

And all three Jackie O's began to walk toward the stage.

Fear pounded in Allie's chest as she climbed the final two steps onto the circular stage, her long-held phobia of a close encounter with Shira bubbling up inside her like a toxic brew. Shira smiled her thin smile at them in return, clapping along with the audience, and slowly the three Jackie O's and the bossy Aussie drew closer together, pulled by the magnetic force of national television. Behind the stage, reflected in flat-panel TV screens hanging in every corner of the room, holograms of the Alpha Academy logo flashed and shimmied, then dissolved into images of Charlie, Skye, and Allie dressed in cute metallic Alphas uniforms, each girl in full makeup with perfect hair. A far cry from the Mojave refugees in poo-brown polyester standing here with Shira.

As she stood under the hot stage lights and clapped robotically along with the studio audience, so much began to make sense to Allie. This explained why Shira was always so worried about the cameras. It wasn't because of her surveillance, or because she cared if the Alphas broke her rules. She didn't care about rules at all. She cared about the networks. Without cameras, there was no show. And without a show, there were no advertisers.

Her smile bigger than ever on the outside, inside Allie began to frantically run through everything she'd done at Alpha Academy. Had all of it been on television? Her legs turned to jelly as she realized everyone at her school had seen her fake her way onto the island by posing as Allie J. They'd seen her horrible public meltdown. Her ridiculous crush on Darwin. The time she purposely sprained her ankle on the track to try to get him to fall for her. And then her next relationship with Mel. Everyone on Earth had seen Mel abandon her in the desert! *Ugh,* Allie thought with a sinking heart. *I'll always be remembered as a wannabe. A wannabe folk singer, a wannabe girlfriend, and a wannabe Alpha.*

Still smiling robotically, Allie blinked back tears. Her acting classes with Careen had taught her this much—what went on in your head didn't have to be what people saw.

"You've figured it out, then?" Shira hissed over the roar of the cameras, finally standing just inches away from Allie.

"Not entirely," Allie smile-clapped, inching closer to the maniacal mogul. "I get that we've been filmed for reality TV. But were we always going to be the last remaining Alphas?"

"Crikey, lolly. Absolutely not. I would have preferred *anyone* else. But for some reason, you three tested the highest with audiences. The networks loved you. Lucky for you, I had no say in the matter."

"And what happened to AJ?" Allie asked through clenched teeth.

"AJ?" Shira shot Allie a blank look. "Oh, you mean the mousy folk singer? I've no clue."

As if on cue, a set of doors in the back of the room opened and AJ vaulted through them, somersaulting straight onto her tiny metallic-skirted rump. The teeny greenie looked as if she had battled a ceiling fan on her way here: Her black hair was matted into a perma-snarl, and her face was streaked with desert dust. She stood up, quickly recovering from her fall, and widened her algae-green eyes, gaping in awe at the enormous crowd. Then she did what any teen celeb would do when faced with a TV audience the size of the population of Delaware. She made a hasty beeline for the stage, her face contorting with forced glee as she barreled toward Shira and the three Jackie O's for her piece of the celebrity pie.

"Shira," Allie whisper-shouted as the crowd roared, "Either she goes or we walk. I mean it. We'd hate to disappoint your sponsors, but . . ."

"Fine," Shira smile-hissed, placing a French-manicured finger on an eraser-sized implant in her ear. "Muses, please escort the PAP saboteur out of the building."

Allie held her breath, waiting to see if Shira's orders would be carried out.

AJ galloped nimbly toward the stage, her eyes glimmering with hope, hungry for attention. But just as she reached the first row, two metallic-clad muses blocked her path, smiling and talking in low voices. Seconds later, they were steering her out of the room, her arms flailing weakly in their iron grip. The odorous yodeler wrenched her head around for one final look at the stage, and her moss-green eyes locked with Allie's navy blue ones. Allie could see her tiny mouth forming words, but the applause was still too loud to hear from so far away. AJ might have been saying *You're dead* or *Love always*— Allie didn't care. She mouthed back *Toodles* and wiggled her long fingers in farewell.

Don't go away angry, AJ. Just go away.

When AJ vanished at last through the Pavilion doors, a half-forgotten feeling settled over Allie like a buttery-soft leather jacket with a flawless fit. Suddenly, Allie felt ah-mazing. Instead of fearful, she felt powerful. Instead of anxious, she felt hopeful. Instead of a nobody, Allie had become a somebody. She might not be an AFL, but she was definitely a VIP.

"Happy?" Shira whispered, her ice-blue eyes searching Allie's face.

"Very," Allie grinned, realizing that things might actually be all right. She reached over and squeezed first Charlie's hand, then Skye's.

"Girls," Shira said, addressing all three of them and gesturing to the audience to quiet their wild applause. "Welcome to the season finale of the most popular new show in America—*Alpha Academy*."

The wave of applause crested again, almost knocking Allie over, and Shira saw her chance to whisper a message to all three girls. She turned off the micro-mic attached to her dress and leaned in. "Thank God it's finally over. A pity you won't be Alphas for life, but I think you'll find this to be a suitable consolation prize. And just think—we're rid of one another, for now."

Allie stomach churned with excitement and nervousness. "For now?" she asked. "Not for ever?"

"Oh, we'll be seeing a lot of each other in future," Shira's ice-blue eyes glittered with a secret behind her sunglasses, and her finger switched her mic back on before traveling to her lips in the universal sign for *shhhh*.

Allie exhaled in exasperation, knowing Shira was wasn't likely to explain herself. She smiled and waved at her parents again, blowing her mom a kiss and vamping for the cameras as a bouncy dance number blared over the applause. Did the tears in her parents' eyes mean she had made them proud, or were they just glad to see her?

Her eyes scanned the huge audience—there were easily three hundred people in the stands, including all the Alphas who'd been kicked out along the way. Everyone was smiling and clapping along to the music. People were starting to stand up and dance. Muses stood every few rows, directing the audience to keep up their cheering.

But then Allie's eyes landed on the most shock-inducing sight yet. More shocking than Shira on the stage alone, more astonishing than the big reveal that they'd been on national television all these weeks.

Standing in one of the rearmost rows of the audience, wearing a TEAM ALLIE A. T-shirt, was a sandy-haired, hazel-eyed boy with Clearasil-perfect skin. He waved wildly at Allie, his arms making huge arcs in the air as he tried to get her attention, his mouth forming the syllables of her name again and again. In the micro-second it took Allie's brain to catch up with her eyes, a wave of adrenaline coursed up her spine with such high-voltage electricity that she inadvertently let out a tiny yelp of surprise.

Fletcher!

21

As the ceiling opened and a shower of glittery confetti and Mylar ALPHAS-emblazoned balloons rained down from above, Skye's stomach thumped dangerously to the beat of the music blaring from hidden speakers. She wondered what the TV producers would do if one of their stars lost her lunch onstage.

Devastation, betrayal, and embarrassment swirled through Skye like the sickening smoothie of hot sauce, raw egg, and pickle juice she'd once drunk on a slumber-party dare in the sixth grade. And just like at the slumber party, this combo was making her want to puke. The theme song to Shira's show (Skye couldn't possibly think of it as *her* show) was set on repeat and Skye danced feebly as she tried not to hurl.

The song was a cheesy cover of the classic wedding hit "We Are Family":

We are family
I got all my Alphas with me!
We are family
Kicking butt at the Academy!

Skye's eyes found Charlie's, and her friend looked as unsure as Skye felt. Only Allie was putting on the perfect show, smiling wide and bobbing along to the music. Charlie's deer-in-headlights face mirrored Skye's insides perfectly.

Just then, the muses standing on either side of the audience began walking toward the stage, signaling that those who wanted to should join them. Skye felt dizzy as the stage crowded with people. The first to find her was Thalia, the house muse for Jackie O. Thalia had always been there for them, like a big sister or a kindly camp counselor, providing an oasis of calm amidst the cutthroat competition of Alpha Academy.

Skye let herself be enveloped by Thalia's lanky basketball-player arms. It was a relief to be supported by someone else's weight, someone she trusted—*wait!* Skye pulled away with a start, realizing that Thalia must have been in on the deception the whole time.

"How could you go along with this?" she whisper-yelled, demanding an explanation from the serene, blond muse. "I thought you were all into honesty and ethics and stuff."

"Some Alphas are born great, some achieve greatness, and some have greatness thrust upon them," Thalia recited in her usual melodic, mellow manner, her golden eyes twinkling under the stage lights. "Shakespeare."

Skye rolled her teal eyes. "If by greatness you mean total humiliation, then yeah."

"I knew you would win," Thalia gushed, ignoring Skye's pout, her own glossed lips curved in a serene smile. "I knew you girls had it. Once you absorb the shock, you'll find fame suits you, Skye. You were born for this." Thalia whispered these final words in Skye's ear like a prophecy, then drifted off to hug Charlie and Allie, her platinum goddess dress flowing around her like she was the Oracle of Delphi.

This kind of fame suits me like a too-small Chanel, Skye quipped inwardly as Thalia moved on. But even if Thalia had lied to them, it was hard to hate a walking, talking self-help manual. And she'd always been right before. Was it possible she was right this time, too? Skye doubted it. She couldn't stop thinking about the fact that she'd been on national TV kissing Syd, eating onions—*ohmuhgod*—even fake-farting! And more recently, getting dissed by Taz after practically throwing herself at him in the middle of the desert. Her stomach churned with the humiliation of it all.

She felt dizzy.

She needed air.

"Skye-high!" chirped the Russian-accented voice of

her mother, former Bolshoi Ballet prima ballerina Natasha Flailenkoff. And suddenly, there she was, her black hair pulled back into a tight, low bun, sashaying toward Skye with the winglike sleeves of her white mohair sweater trailing dramatically behind her over a black unitard, her deep-set blue eyes moist and shining.

"Our little TV star," cried her father, his voice husky with emotion. He trailed behind Natasha, unbuttoning his gray jacket as he opened his arms to hug his only daughter. "We missed you."

"Mom, Dad!" Skye whirled around just as both her parents reached her, and the three of them collided in a Hamilton family hug that was tighter than spandex shorts on Jonah Hill.

The moment Skye breathed in her mother's Eau d'Issey and her father's woodsy aftershave, she knew her battle to keep her composure was hopelessly lost. The tears came fast and furious, like the first moments of the Log Jam ride at Six Flags Great Adventure. She choked out a few hasty sobs and buried her face in her mom's huge sweater, feeing instantly better. Just as fast as her crying jag had started, it faded away.

"Don't cry, Minka," her mother said, using her daughter's Russian pet name and squeezing Skye's shaking hands in her ring-encrusted ones, her diamond tennis bracelet falling against Skye's wrist. "You did it! You were one of the last Alphas standing. You should be proud." Her mother's sculpted features softened into a reassuring smile.

"But how could they film me for TV without my knowledge? Isn't that illegal?" Skye squeaked, ignoring her parents' loving words. Maybe if she could erase half of what she'd done in front of the cameras, she could be proud. For now, she was still more shaken than a virgin mango-tini.

Skye's dad pulled a folded piece of paper out of the breast pocket of his suit jacket. "After you left for Alpha Academy, they informed us that it was a TV show. We were shocked that it happened without you knowing, but the admission papers had a clause specifying Brazille Industries' right to all video taken on the island, so legal recourse was out . . ."

"Oh," Skye said in a small voice. "Guess I should have read what I was signing."

"But then," Skye's mom continued breathlessly, "we saw the show. The island looked so incredible, and you were learning so much. We didn't want to pull you out of all that."

"We had Sleeves fan clubs making pilgrimages to Body Alive!" her father said, his gray eyes twinkling with pride. "Mom's studio enrollment has quadrupled. Every little girl in the country wants to be the next Skye Hamilton."

Fan clubs? The next Skye Hamilton?

Skye shot a doubting look at her parents. They couldn't possibly be serious. Could they?

"Your mother and I are so proud of you, and of what you've become. You're a household name."

Skye blinked hard and shook her head, barely able to process what her father was saying. Of its own accord, her dancer's body formed a deep plié and wound up in a curtsey, as if she were bowing after a performance of *Swan Lake*. Had Alphas actually been Skye's best performance yet? It was starting to seem that way.

Maybe it made some sort of sense. After all, everyone loved an underdog. Skye had started at Alpha Academy as a big fish from a small pond, the best dancer in Westchester. That was before she'd had to compete with the best dancers on Earth, every single one of them better and more disciplined than she was. She'd been knocked off her pedestal early, and through sheer will had managed to pull herself back up.

She nodded slowly, reframing her time at the Academy in less mortifying terms. She'd gotten tougher, improved her craft, and—maybe most important of all—learned to balance ballet and boys.

"I guess I can see how it would make for a fun TV show," Skye said cautiously, the theme music blaring above the stage reaching a crescendo. "We've all grown up a little."

"Girls everywhere look up to you, Skye. After you hurt your ankle, you were determined to get better. And you did! You got better than Triple. The HAD slipper worked," her mother whispered. Natasha smiled, raising her eyebrows knowingly.

My HAD slipper! Skye felt another lurching sensation in

191

her stomach. What if some producer had tossed the precious slipper away, not realizing it was Skye's good luck charm and a family heirloom? The slipper had gotten her mother the prima ballerina spot in the Bolshoi Ballet, and she'd entrusted it to Skye once her daughter had been admitted into the Academy.

But just as Skye was about to flee the stage and go find it, Natasha opened her purse and pulled out the soft pink toe shoe. "They gave us a tour of the dorms. I thought you might want to see this again."

"Thanks," Skye managed, taking the slipper and putting it to her nose. The lavender-scented slips of paper she'd carefully written her hopes and dreams (HADs) on still had some herbal essence left in them. For the life of her, she couldn't remember what her HADs had been, other than the most important:

Survive Alpha Academy. Be the last girl standing.

Check and check.

Maybe her parents were right to be proud. Skye straightened her posture and took a deep breath, shoving the purple toe shoe into the cargo pocket of her Wilderness Girl shorts. She'd figure out what her new HADs would be once she got home.

For now, there was one more person she needed to see.

"Can I meet back up with you in a few minutes?" she asked her parents. They nodded, already sucked into a conversation with Thalia and a few other muses.

Skye patted her pocket, a smile playing on her lips, and began to move through the crowd, her steps long and graceful again now that she wasn't in danger of shock-vomming all over the stage.

Her eyes scanned the audience dancing in the aisles, searching for the Brazille brothers. At last she spotted Taz, giving an interview to a perky brunette woman who waved an E! Entertainment microphone under his chiseled chin. A cameraman stood nearby, recording Taz's impressions of the show. *Of my show*, Skye thought, laughing at how weird the phrase sounded in her brain.

"I had no idea!" Taz was saying. "I was just as shocked as the girls were. My mom's always been a pretty good lia—uh, secret keeper, but this time she took it to a whole new level. Wait, is this live? Can you edit that last part?" Taz's arctic-blue eyes flirt-pleaded with the E! reporter.

"No problem, Taz. As long you answer one more question everyone's dying to know the answer to: What's going to happen between you and Skye now that that the show's over?"

Great question!

Skye's breath caught in her throat as she waited for Taz to formulate a sound bite for the camera. But then she exhaled, realizing she didn't need to wait for Taz to decide. Skye already knew in her gut what she wanted.

"Uh, I guess we'll find out," Taz stammered, his face turning red. Skye wondered if he was feeling guilty about leaving her and running onto the peanut plane, or if it was the fact that now Skye was every bit as much of a celeb as he was?

Doesn't matter, Skye decided, unconsciously shaking her head to push the questions out of her mind.

When Taz's interview was over, Skye leapt up the three stairs that still separated her from the darkest-haired, bluest-eyed Brazille boy.

"Hey," she said, smiling neutrally.

"Hey yourself," Taz answered, his blush still lingering on his cheeks as if he'd just been shoveling snow. *Still cute*, Skye sighed inwardly.

"So . . . you had no idea? About the show?" Skye steadied herself, placing one hand on a smooth white seatback and balancing on both toes. She wondered how long it had been since she'd practiced an actual ballet routine.

"None. No way. I can't believe it," Taz grinned. "I hear you three are world-famous now."

"I'll have to get back to you on that one," Skye grinned, getting ready to drop a little guilt-bomb on the conversation. "I wonder what the audience thought of you and Mel leaving us on that mountain in the desert."

"That was"—Taz paused and lowered his voice to a whisper—"totally accidental. I'm not, you know, *that guy*."

"Not usually, you mean," Skye said lightly. The two feet between them still vibrated with a certain unfinished *something*. But she needed to figure out her next steps by herself. On her own. No strings attached.

If it was meant to be with Taz, they'd have a whole lifetime to find out. For now, she reassured herself, she wanted to live her life as Skye Solo, not Taz-manian Skye.

Taz grinned back. "Not *usually*. Yeah. And it'll never happen again."

"I'm sure it won't," she nodded. She leaned up toward him and pecked him quickly on the cheek, first checking to see if any cameras were pointed their way. This was one farewell kiss she wanted to keep private. "Keep in touch, okay?" she whispered.

"That's it?" Taz asked, his thick eyebrows shooting into the air like two sides of a shocked parenthesis. "Should I text you?"

"Probably not," Skye shrugged. "I just want to dance and de-Alphatize for a while."

"Cool," Taz smiled, reaching out a strong hand and putting it gently on Skye's toned shoulder. "Good luck. Not that you need it."

"You too," Skye grinned, waving goodbye for now.

Having finished her Taz-manian interlude, Skye pirouetted her way across the aisles to join the gaggle of bun-heads she'd spotted. Tweety, Prue, and Sadie grabbed her in a noisy four-way hug, shrieking with excitement and bubbling over with Alphas gossip.

"You did it, girl!" yelled Prue. "If it couldn't be me, I'm glad it was you."

"Mimi's totally taking all the credit," winked Sadie, her red hair tucked up into the classic ballerina bun they all wore during rehearsals. "I heard she taped the *Tyra* show yesterday, billed as Alpha Academy's genius choreographer."

Skye grinned, overwhelmed by how ah-mazing it was to be back with her fellow dancers. "I can't wait to see Mimi," she said sarcastically. "Or maybe I can."

"I was on *Tyra*, too," someone said behind her. Skye knew that voice. Perfect pitch. Perfect tone. TV-ready.

Triple!

Skye whirled around and found herself staring at Trip's high cheekbones, gorgeous catlike eyes, and flawless blowout. "Yo, Sleeves. You did it. You're welcome." Triple's perfectly plucked eyebrows arched ironically. She was wearing a strapless white tulip dress that seemed to float over her gorgeous figure. Next to Trip, Skye felt like a dowdy postal worker. But she didn't care. She opened her arms wide and gave Triple the bear hug to end all bear hugs, even though Trip hated to be touched. After all, if not for Triple, Skye's dancing would never have improved. And she would have never won the regatta race.

"Thanks, Trip," Skye grinned as Triple shook her off. "You were my ultimate inspiration."

"Yeah, yeah." Trip eye-rolled, her full lips pout-smiling in spite of having lost. "I live to serve. Luckily, for whatever reason, I got a lot of airtime. I just inked a deal for a spin-off show—*Triple's House of Pain*. It's a makeover show for Betas, where I turn them from losers into . . . well, into me."

Ha! Skye nodded, making a mental note to warn all her friends back in Westchester not to audition, but knowing she'd never miss an episode. "Congrats. Sounds Trip-tastic."

"And what are you going to do now, Skye?" Prue interrupted. "I mean, you can kind of do whatever you want now."

"First, I'm going to change out of these clothes," Skye joked. "And then, we'll see. I'll go wherever my toe shoes take me . . ."

"Um, Sleeves?" Triple interrupted. She never did have much patience for other people talking, Skye remembered. "I was kind of watching you and Taz before. Are you guys . . . ?"

"Taz is officially single," laughed Skye. "Trip, you should go talk to him. My sloppy seconds are like most people's firsts."

Her former frenemy executed a classic Trip hair-flip-disdainful-snort combo, and all the bun-heads cracked up as she flounced away.

Even though she was in a crowded room with cameras everywhere, Skye realized, she hadn't felt so free in months. Skye reached for the ballet slipper in her pocket, her fingers worrying the shoe's frayed satin edge as she sealed her next HAD in her mind:

Embrace whatever comes next. You've earned it.

22

THE PAVILION
HALF MOON THEATER
NOVEMBER 4TH
7:15 P.M.

"Don't forget to pack all my Alphas clothes from the closet marked *Allie A!*" Allie yelled to the departing backs of her parents. Felicia and Fred Abbott had spent fifteen minutes gushing to Allie about her newfound acting talent, then another ten telling her how amazed they were that the Wilderness Girls made a nature warrior out of their little germaphobe. Now they were headed to Jackie O to pack up her stuff, and she promised to meet them in front of the Pavilion after she said goodbye to the O's.

Allie stood at the edge of the stage, wondering if the Purell corporation would make her their official spokesperson after all the free advertising she'd given them, when she saw Mel's face break through the crowd.

A familiar flutter of butterflies shot through her stomach the way it always did when she saw Mel's lantern jaw, intense green eyes, and thatch of floppy white-blond hair, but when he put his arms around her, the flutter suddenly died out. Allie felt . . . nothing. Nothing but an intense urge to get away from him.

Mel smiled. "I missed you."

Allie tried to think of something sweet to say back, but no words came. She smile-nodded, buying time as she tried to figure out how her heart could be in direct opposition to her eyes. Mel was so cute. He dressed so well. And they'd been through so much together, especially since the PAP crash.

But the disappointing facts were suddenly all too obvious: No matter how cute Mel might be, Allie just didn't respect him anymore. Not after what he did on the plateau.

She pursed her rosebud lips, and gave her heart one last chance to embrace the handsome Brazille boy in front of her. But no matter how much her head knew the harmony to this love song, Allie's heart refused to sing the Mel-ody.

Finally, she opened her mouth to inform Mel that her feelings had changed. But just as she was about to utter the words, her navy blue eyes caught sight of Fletcher making his way toward them. Running, actually. Still wearing his dumb TEAM ALLIE A. T-shirt.

Oops. Allie jumped from one foot to the other, not relishing the idea of these two meeting each other. She'd been so busy trying to dump Mel that she'd momentarily forgotten Fletcher was here with his own Allie-related agenda.

"What's *he* doing here?" Fletcher panted when he finally reached them, his model-perfect hazel eyes jumping from Allie to Mel and back again.

"I'm her boyfriend. Where else would I be?" Mel said, speaking as though talking to a child. He moved closer to Allie, encircling her shoulders with one arm as always, then turned to glare at Fletcher. "And you are?"

Allie shook Mel off and took a step away, not wanting the cameras to get the wrong idea. *Wouldn't want the world thinking I'm still Mel's girlfriend when nothing could be further from the truth.* If only she could get around to telling him that.

"I was sort of hoping I could be your boyfriend again," Fletcher said, his neck reddening as he boxed Mel out by stepping between him and Allie. "Your desert adventure aired last night. I saw the way he just left you there, Allie. Not cool. Not cool at all."

Fletcher's hazel eyes widened as he shook his head, silently communicating the obvious next line in his train of thought: *Not as cool as me.* Allie gaped in stunned silence. She was more floored than parquet.

Fletcher's chin-dimple was as cute as ever. His teeth were so white they were practically blue. And those eyes. As Allie gazed into them, she was almost transported back to the months she'd spent praying his gaze would return to her, instead of looking into the far less vibrant eyes of her former best friend.

And now here he was, giving Allie his full attention. Wearing the dorky fan-shirt they were selling in the stands. Stepping up to tabloid sensation Mel Brazille to reclaim his title as Allie's boyfriend. The whole situation was so ridiculous, Allie couldn't help but laugh. As she shook with giggles, laugh-tears formed in the corners of her eyes and dripped down the sides of her sunburned face.

Finally, she wiped away a couple of tears and cleared her throat. "Fletch, wow. What about Trina? When I left, you two were inseparable."

"Trina?" Fletcher looked surprised and confused, as if he had to struggle to remember who Allie was talking about.

"Yeah, remember? You locked lips on the Finding Nemo ride with my former best friend? It was kind of the reason we broke up?" Allie asked impatiently. Mel was getting antsy, looking at his watch and then back at Allie, waiting for her to fire Fletcher.

"Right." Fletcher looked a bit embarrassed. "Trina and I broke up. I became sort of obsessed with watching the show. Allie, you were so . . . amazing! I didn't know you had so much in you. The acting, the AJ impersonations, the tight uniforms. All of it. I was hooked. I mean, I know it's been a while, but I thought . . ." He grinned at her hopefully, flashing a row of those perfect teeth.

Allie nodded on the outside but cringed on the inside. Fletcher's words just seemed empty and hollow. He was right about one thing: She did have a lot inside of her. Too much to waste on Fletcher, the boy who had once confessed that gelling his hair took him thirty-five minutes every morning. Allie opened her mouth to tell him, but just then she noticed a group of men and women in expensive-looking suits, each one typing on a smartphone and periodically glancing over at her. They were huddled in a cluster, and seemed to be inching nearer. When she looked over at them, they waved eagerly, beckoning her their way.

Great, what next? Was this the FBI, ready to prosecute her for identity theft? Or maybe it was AJ's publicity team, preparing to sue Allie for slander or defamation. Allie smiled nervously at them and held up her index finger to indicate she'd be over in a minute.

"Al, come on, haven't you wasted long enough listening to this pathetic ex of yours?" Mel piped up, reaching out to grab Allie's arm.

The three of them stood facing one another, a love triangle waiting to explode.

Allie stared from one boy to the other. Mel was the taller and blonder of the two, while Fletcher had more toned abs and smaller pores. But neither one held the slightest appeal for the new, post-desert version of Allie A. Abbott.

She sigh-groaned in frustration, realizing she would actually prefer be talking to the FBI and moving on with her life than standing here looking at these two for another minute. They had more in common with each other than they did with her. They could discuss the Clinique men's skincare line, the latest Banana Republic catalogue, and their modeling careers.

Two of the prettiest boys on the planet, and I don't want either one. It was like walking through the aisles of a Whole Foods when you'd just finished Thanksgiving dinner. The produce was beautiful, but you couldn't possibly imagine eating it.

Two sets of expectant eyes stared at her impatiently. Allie had to tell them.

"Actually," she said, her navy blue eyes bouncing from one handsome face to the other like a metronome, "neither of you are my boyfriend."

"You can't be serious," Mel cried. "Look, I'm sorry about the plane. I was about to go back for you, I swear—"

Fletcher cut Mel off. "Al, we have so much history. I get you. I know where you come from. Come on, babe, we look so perfect together. Remember how people used to ask us if we were cousins?"

Allie backed away from the metrosexual duo. "I just need to be single right now. Maybe you can help each other heal. I smell a bro-mance brewing!"

"It's my new signature scent," Fletcher admitted. "I made it myself at a kiosk in the mall. You like it?"

Allie whirled on her heel and walked away without another word. She was free! At least free for the moment, until these lawyer/undercover cops/publicity managers sank their hooks into her. She took a deep breath, relieved not to have Fletcher's manufactured musk or Mel's scented Aveda pomade flooding her nostrils. The smell of funky Wilderness Girl outfit, dust, river mud, and independence was all she needed.

She took out her bottle of Purell and squirted it on her hands, just as a helmet-haired woman approached her. "I'm Lucinda Saint John. I represent actors and entertainers, including Anne Hathaway, Kristen Stewart, Lea Michele, and both Taylors—Swift and Lautner."

"Hi," Allie said, avoiding her germy extended hand. Who knew where those celebrities had been?

"I want to represent you. You don't know this yet, but you're the It Girl, Allie, and you're about to receive dozens of offers from directors who want to work with you."

Ohmuhgod. Allie pinched the inside of her arm just to make sure she wasn't dreaming.

"You want to be my agent," Allie breathed. Suddenly, the room began to spin. So this is what it's like to have your dreams start coming true, she thought. "I think I need to sit down." *Actually, I think I might pass out.*

Helmet-Hair nodded kindly, dragging a folding chair over to Allie. "Please, sit down. You look a little pale. Can I offer you a Luna bar? Yesterday in the desert you were jonesing for one."

Allie gave the woman a stunned smile and accepted the bar.

As Allie devoured the chocolate caramel Luna, she closed her eyes and tried to absorb this moment. She'd thrown away two model-perfect boyfriends and gained a potential acting career. Not bad for a girl who lied her way onto the show. Not bad at all.

Catching sight of her parents drifting back over, dragging two huge suitcases behind them, she turned to Lucinda Saint John and smiled, her mouth full of Luna and her heart full of hope. "Where do I sign?"

Life was starting to taste as sweet as the caramel on her tongue.

23

Charlie leaned against a wall near the theater doors, watching the crowd still gathered onstage as the *Alpha Academy* theme song wound down. Former Alphas milled around with parents and producers, everyone's hair flecked with shiny A-shaped confetti. Shira stood in the center of the stage haggling with two men dressed in black, their heads strapped into headphone mics. Camera operators still dipped and swerved, focusing their lenses on the reuniting students for a few final shots.

Charlie's espresso-bean eyes sought out her two cargo-shorted besties. Just like her, Allie and Skye had survived to the end of the line, and just like her, they were still piecing together what "winning" Shira's game actually meant. Charlie's mouth lifted in a smile when she spotted Allie thumbing through a sheaf of documents produced from the briefcase of a woman in a business suit, her parents standing awkwardly behind her and guarding two massive rolling suitcases. Charlie smiled, knowing what was inside—as many heat-activated Alphas outfits as Allie could carry.

A light bulb went on in Charlie's head when she thought about those clothes. *Shira's going to make millions on Alphas merchandise*. Charlie shook her head and snickered as she put the pieces together. The whole island would probably turn into a Shira-run eco-resort after the show was over. Charlie had to hand it to Shira, she'd thought of everything. Even sneaking into the control room to disable the surveillance cameras, Charlie hadn't a clue that the footage was fed via satellite to a production team.

Charlie looked back at the stage and searched out Skye. She spotted her platinum wavelets flipping in the center of the stage as she demonstrated a hip-hop-meets-salsa routine for her mother, a gorgeous woman with jet-black hair and a dramatically flowing cardigan wrapped around her sculpted torso. Skye's father, a handsome salt-and-pepper-haired guy in a gray suit, looked on admiringly.

Watching her friends not just coping but *enjoying* the end of Shira's insane competition, Charlie's feelings of dismay and victimhood began to peel off her like an exfoliating mud mask. She may have sacrificed a lot to be an unwitting star of *Alpha Academy*—her dignity, her pride, and her privacy, for starters—but she'd also won the biggest prize of all: true friendship.

Just as this thought came to her, both Skye and Allie glanced up, their eyes finding Charlie's. She wave-smiled back at them, relieved to know that no matter what direction their lives took now, they would always be linked by what they'd gone through on Alpha Island and in the Mojave.

Which was pretty awesome for a girl like Charlie. Before Alphas, the only people she had ever really trusted were Darwin and her mom.

Thinking about her mom sent a lonesome pang rippling through Charlie's chest, an ache for Bee and her perfect British propriety, her generous way of seeing everything. Yet again, Charlie scanned the dwindling crowd in the vain hope of spotting her mother, searching the empty audience seats for Bee's reassuring presence. But of course Bee wasn't here. Shira would never allow her back on the island she'd helped to engineer—they'd struck a deal, after all. Probably a whole clause about it in Shira's contract with the TV studio.

Just as Charlie felt a lump of self-pity sticking in the back of her throat like peanut butter, her aPod vibrated.

Bee: I'm sorry I can't be there, Charlie, but I'm so proud of you! And I'll see you sooner than you think!

PS: I figured out how to watch the show on my computer in London—give a kiss to Allie and Skye for me. Thank goodness you three made up.

Ha! Charlie grinned down at her phone. In a way, Bee had been there with her the whole time, through the miracle of TV. *Guess I should thank Shira for that,* Charlie caught herself thinking. She shook her head slightly, knowing she wasn't about to thank Shira for anything. Not after what she'd put them through. *Not gonna happen.*

Charlie wondered what Bee meant about seeing her soon. Would Charlie have to get on a plane and fly to England? Was Bee going to meet her back in New Jersey, where they had family? She twirled her cameo bracelets absently, not having a clue what her next move would be. Maybe Shira would have a message from her mom.

When Charlie looked up from her phone, Skye and Allie were both motioning for her to come join them onstage.

Just a minute, Charlie mouthed. She'd spotted three fish out of water hustling toward her, making a beeline for the door. She stepped in front of Tiger, Ember, and Mountain and blocked their path. "Sneaking out?" she smiled.

"Yeah. After a month in Mojave, this place is making us a little claustrophobic," Tiger grinned, her skin still glowing from the peat-moss botanical soak Allie had concocted for her makeover. "But they told us we couldn't fly home until they were done filming. Nice win." Tiger's clear brown eyes sparkled with pride under the stage lights.

"The uniforms looked good on you guys," Ember added shyly.

"We couldn't have done it without you," Charlie grinned. But then a creepy suspicion tickled the corners of her mind. "Did you know about the show?"

"Of course." Mountain said. "Did you seriously think there was such a thing as the Wilderness Girls? Were all actors, wired with cameras. We were hired to play Girl Scouts, but the organization tried to sue so we made up this whole WG thing. Norwegian knife. Ha! That was an ad lib."

Charlie giggled. "I'll miss you."

Tiger was inching toward the door, probably desperate to put on some jeans. "Let's plan a reunion trip for next year. Maybe a spa."

Charlie laugh-nodded, embracing all three WGs in a group hug. "Sounds great. I'll start working on Allie and Skye now."

"Tell them congrats for us," Ember said. "And goodbye for now."

And then all three girls hustled through the electric doors, leaving nothing but the smell of sage, peat moss, and a job well done in their wake.

Charlie turned away from the door to join Allie and Skye

onstage, but now it was her turn to have her path blocked. Darwin stood squarely in front of her, his hands held out wide for a hug and a cinnamon-scented toothpick dangling from his kissable lips This was one blockade she would be happy to stop for.

"There you are!" Darwin's deep voice breathed in her ear as he pulled her to him.

"Hi," she whisper-grinned. "I was wondering when you'd come find me."

"Listen, Charlie," Darwin stammered, pulling away with a worried look in his hazel eyes. Charlie blinked, furrowing her brow as she waited for him to continue, noticing her boyfriend had dark circles under his eyes. "I swear, I had no idea this was happening. I've been worried sick and doing everything I could to get you guys back sooner. And I'm just as shocked as you about this whole TV thing. As soon as I can get my mom alone, I'm going to open up a can of—"

Charlie silenced him with another huge hug, squeezing him with all her malnourished might. She would never suspect Darwin of knowing about the TV show. There was no way he'd be able to keep that kind of secret from her—he'd always been a blabbermouth.

"Don't worry," she murmured in his warm ear, enjoying her surfer boyfriend's beachy smell. "And I'm the one who's sorry, D. I was a total jerk on the plateau, and even before that. You've been nothing but patient with me. Whatever happens now, you'll always be my angelfish."

She pulled her head back to look into Darwin's hazel eyes. When their eyes met, Charlie knew that wherever she was headed, *he* was her home.

"I love you, too," he said softly. "I don't know what I would have done if . . . if those nature girls hadn't been there and something had happened—"

Charlie put a grubby finger on his puffy pink lips, then plucked out his toothpick. She didn't want to think about what-ifs right now. But then she decided she had a better way to keep Darwin quiet.

Charlie stood on tiptoe and leaned in to plant her lips on Darwin's, finally feeling safe and secure after so many weeks of being panicked and afraid.

For once, Charlie didn't care if Shira saw, if the cameras captured this kiss and broadcasted it to the entire world. It was time the world knew, anyway: She and Darwin weren't just an Alpha Island romance. They were forever. She was more certain of this than she was about anything else. She may not have a home to go back to or parents standing here to help guide her next steps, but she did have an ah-mazing boyfriend.

"Charlie Deery?" a voice cut in on her cinematic kiss. Charlie's eyes fluttered open in irritation and she reluctantly detached her lips from Darwin's. Two men in crisp black suits stood just behind Darwin, their hands both clasped in front of them. Both wore aviator sunglasses and close-cropped haircuts. Their jaws were sharp enough to cut glass.

"That's me," Charlie cleared her throat, moving to stand beside Darwin. She reached up and nervously twirled a strand of her mahogany hair, unsure of what was happening. Hadn't she had enough surprises for one day?

"We'd like you to come with us," Suit #1 said.

"Um . . . I didn't catch your names," Charlie stalled. She checked Darwin's face to see if he was in on this, but he just shrugged his shoulders and flicked his eyes back to the suits, waiting for an explanation. Like her, he hadn't the slightest idea what they wanted.

"Don't be alarmed, Miss Deery," Suit #2 said. "We think you're going to like where you're headed."

"Which is?" Darwin asked, unable to keep the suspicion out of his voice as he straightened his posture, pulling himself up to his full six feet.

Charlie stood waiting, her stomach suddenly colonized by a flock of bird-flu carrying butterflies. *This is what spending too much time with Shira Brazille does to a girl*, she thought.

"The White House," said Suit #1 quietly, beaming a businesslike micro-smile at Charlie.

Ohmuhgod. Charlie's panic vanished instantly, replaced by rainbow-colored fizzy excitement. Talk about meeting an Alpha for life! The White House was like the Alpha mother ship, and Charlie was being invited aboard. Her heart beat with happy anticipation as she turned to look at Darwin. His eyes were round as dinner plates, piled high with equal helpings of shock and pride.

"Holy crap!" he cried as he grabbed her in a congratulatory headlock.

Charlie leaned on Darwin for support—her legs had turned to Jell-O. Was this really happening? "Seriously?" she whisper-asked the black suits. "Is this a joke?"

"No joke, Miss Deery. The Presidential Office of Technological Advancement has been paying close attention to your little TV show. Whatever you did impressed the hell out of them, and they want to offer you a job."

Charlie's mouth lifted into a dazed smile of disbelief as her brown eyes drifted over the heads of the black suits and searched out the person that had made this all possible. Did Shira know about this? If not, Charlie couldn't wait to tell her. Because in spite of all the mind games the glossy Aussie had subjected them to, Charlie now believed Shira really did want her girls to find success.

Her eyes finally found Shira, and she was shocked to discover the mogul had raised her trademark black sunglasses a little and was aiming her ice-blue eyes directly at Charlie in a wide-eyed stare full of unspoken expectation, mixed— Charlie was sure of it—with a twinkle that could only be called *pride*. Charlie winked, then she mouthed two words that, until now, she'd never actually meant when it came to Shira. *Thank you.*

But the Aussie just shrugged, as if to say "Don't thank me, lolly, thank yourself," before her jewel-encrusted hand lowered her black sunglasses back over her eyes.

A shiver-inducing realization hit Charlie: *Someday soon, I might be in a position to grant Shira Brazille a favor.* She swallowed a laugh. How much things had changed since the day she begged Shira to let her join the Academy!

Turning back to Darwin, Charlie pushed the thought to the back of her mind for now. "Okay, D. I think this officially means you don't have to yell at your mom about the whole TV show thing."

"Hmm, I'll think about that one," Darwin answered.

"Hate to break this up, Miss Deery, but we have a plane waiting," Suit #1 interrupted.

"But . . . what about him?" Charlie stammered, placing a proprietary hand on Darwin.

"Just go," Darwin said. "I'll find you soon. I always do."

Charlie's head spun. She had just reunited with Darwin, and now they were already being ripped apart? *No way. If I'm really an Alpha now, then I get to call the shots.*

"No." Charlie pulled her shoulders back and stood facing the black suits with her game face on, prepared to do some bargaining. "I'll go on one condition. He comes with me." She pointed her thumb at the airspace next to Darwin.

The black suits looked at each other and then back at Charlie. They shrugged like two people who were in no position to argue.

Charlie grinned. Shira was right after all—some things were better than winning.

EPILOGUE

"Looks like a full house," Skye murmured to herself as she stared at the flat-screen monitors on each wall of the greenroom of the Kodak Theater. Any minute now the three winning Alphas would be reunited onstage with Shira Brazille for the *Alpha Academy Reunion Special*. At least a thousand people were seated in the audience, all of them waiting to see the Jackie O's confrontation with their former principal. Leo Vanderbees, the host of such reality mega-hits as *School Spirit Faceoff*, *She Stole My Boyfriend*, *Shopping with the Stars*, and now the *Alpha Academy* spinoff hit *Project Beta: Triple's House of Pain*, walked into the room trailing the scent of John Varvatos cologne and brandishing his ubiquitous uber-white smile.

Skye jumped up from the white leather couch she was perched on. "Hi, Mr. Vanderbees," she managed, trying not to act too starstruck. After all, as she'd come to understand over the past few months, she was a pretty huge star her-self. She'd taken to wearing wigs and dark glasses on her commute from Westchester into midtown Manhattan, where the New York Ballet Academy was located, so that she could have some peace and anonymity on the train. She was tired of answering endless questions about how to get onto *Alpha Academy 2* or whether Taz was a good kisser.

"Skye, you look even more gorge in person. Please, call me Leo," Vanderbees said, still smiling his ridiculously toothy smile. Skye wondered if his face ever relaxed, or if he'd had it injected to stay smiling even when he slept.

"Thanks," she said, twirling slightly in the sparkly white corset she'd paired with a pink silk tulip skirt. She'd com-pleted the ensemble with a pair of fuchsia silk arm-sleeves, a look that had always been her trademark in the studio but that, thanks to the TV show, was now a mega-trend around the country.

She had to agree, she *was* looking pretty "gorge." Her favorite teacher at the New York Ballet Academy, Hungarian ballet legend Ilona Sandinski, had gone with her and her mother to find the outfit at Bergdorf's, and all three of them thought it showed off her more-sculpted-than-ever shoul-der and back muscles but still made her look elegant. She leaned over and snuck in a few shoulder stretches before showtime. Her muscles were sore from the long plane ride, or maybe it was the eight-hour day of ballet practice she had missed yesterday in order to get here.

Vanderbees looked at his watch and shot his eyes toward the door just as it opened to reveal a distracted Charlie, furiously typing on her BlackBerry. Before Charlie was properly inside the room, Vanderbees jumped up and ran to shake her hand.

"Charlie, Leo Vanderbees. Looking forward to interviewing you. But just a quick clarification, my notes tell me you're not willing to say *anything* about what you're doing now. True?" Vanderbees kept smiling, but his pale gray eyes flickered with concern.

Charlie pushed a few final buttons on her BlackBerry, pursed her glossed lips and shook her head. "The project's top secret. That's all I can say at this time." She turned to greet Skye and her big brown eyes lit up, still pure Charlie even if her exterior looked wildly different from the girl in cargo shorts and a sunburn Skye had said goodbye to at the Pavilion six months before.

"Skye, that dress is incredible!" Charlie said by way of a greeting.

"Thanks!" Skye squealed. "You look great, too. So professional."

Charlie wore a black Rag and Bone pantsuit with a crisp white button-down underneath. Her makeup was minimal, and her straight brown hair was wrapped up in a polished

French twist. The diamond A pendant Allie had sent them both dangled at her collarbone, just like the one Skye wore around her neck. The pendant had arrived a month ago at Skye's house with a note from an excited Allie about having landed her first big TV role.

Charlie pulled Skye toward her for an excited hug. "Thank goodness you made it!" she squealed. "I was worried I'd have to face Shira alone. Now we just need Al."

As if on cue, the greenroom door opened again and there she was, dressed in strappy heels and a midnight blue one-shoulder minidress. Allie A. Abbott, better known to most by her starring role as Elinor Dashwood, from the hit CW show *Jane Austen Junior High*, stepped into the room and paused to stare happily at her best friends.

Her hair was dyed a bit lighter than her usual honey-blond and her makeup was stage-perfect—she rocked some seriously smoky eyes and her cheeks glowed with iridescent blush—but otherwise Allie looked just the same. Except, Skye noted, happier and way more confident.

Come to think of it, Skye realized as her teal eyes flicked from Allie to Charlie to the greenroom mirror, they *all* did.

Allie's perfect ski-slope nose wrinkled with joy. "Ohmuhgod!" she screamed.

"Allie!" Charlie cried.

"Group hug!" the three girls shouted simultaneously.

Finally, Skye thought as she struggled for air while squeezing Allie and Charlie, *we're all together again.*

Just one more piece of the puzzle missing.

"We all look ah-mazing," Allie sighed, smiling at her besties when they finally broke free of their group hug. "Can you believe it's already been six months?"

"Kinda, yeah," Charlie said. "It feels like a lifetime ago already."

"I know," Skye agreed, rotating her ankles to stay limber before they were called to the stage. "But I still have flashbacks sometimes."

"Me too," Allie nodded. "At least once a week, I wake up thinking Shira's about to bust me."

"Save it for the show!" Vanderbees boomed, interrupting their pre-reunion reunion. "This is solid gold TV. Let's keep it fresh for the viewers. Allie, quick question for my notes—are you still with that boyfriend who tried to get you back after the show? What was his name?"

"Fletcher," all three girls answered.

"And no, she's totally not," Charlie offered. "By the way, Darwin just texted me. He says hi."

"Hi, Darwin! Hang on, I used to know someone named Fletcher?" Allie asked, faux-innocently blinking her long black lashes.

"I read in *Us Weekly* that you were dating your costar," Skye said in a deep, mock-Vanderbees voice as she waved an imaginary mic under Allie's pointy chin. "True or false?"

"I'm dating around," Allie announced, as if they didn't speak every day. "Why tie myself down to just one hottie, right?"

"Enough!" Leo interrupted again. "Wait until we roll camera."

"Okay, Leo," Skye eye-rolled, and she was about to add *If we know anything, it's how to make great TV*, when Shira walked into the room through a separate entrance Skye hadn't noticed before.

"G'day, lollies," she said, whipping off a black trench coat and tossing an enormous Dior bag onto the greenroom couch as she stalked over to the mirror. "Glad you could make it."

"Turns out this was in our contract," eye-rolled Allie, "so, like, we kind of had to make it."

"Indeed it was," Shira nodded as she peered into the mirror and arranged her auburn curls, her dark sunglasses hiding her eyes. In the mirror's reflection, her blood-red lips curled at the corners the way they did when she was about to drop a bombshell. "But this is the last *Alpha Academy* appearance you have to make until we start shooting *Alpha Academy 2*. And then, of course, we'll need you to model Brazille Enterprises clothing and makeup for the ad campaign. We've already got a line of Allie A. hair products in production, as well as Charlie denim and Skye dancewear."

"She owns our images in perpetuity," Charlie informed Skye and Allie, her voice weary as she typed on her BlackBerry. "Also in the contract."

Skye felt the same old half-sick, half-giddy fizzing in her stomach that being in a room with Shira always brought on. The phrase *She owns our images in perpetuity* echoed in her ears, but she tried to put it out of her mind. Tonight, she would hop a plane to England to play the part of the Black Swan in the London Ballet's *Swan Lake*. She had made it; her hopes and dreams were coming true. All because of Shira.

"Oh, Charlie, always so focused on the tiniest details!" Shira smirked, snapping a Chanel compact shut and whirling around to face the room. "We'll talk about this later. Leo, I believe it's time we took the stage. America is waiting!"

"Right, Ms. Brazille." Leo jumped up, instantly animated like a marionette for whom Shira held the strings. "Showtime, ladies."

"Let's go out together," Skye whispered to Allie and Charlie as they walked down the hall behind Shira's clicking stilettos.

The three girls grabbed hands at the edge of the stage, where an enormous A-shaped couch awaited the stars of *Alpha Academy* and their host.

Skye sucked in her breath and smiled, her body tingling with pre-stage jitters. She looked to her right at Charlie, then at Allie on her left, remembering the last time they'd held hands like this—outside the Pavilion, when they were just three exhausted friends hoping to catch a break and beat a sneaky saboteur back home.

"And one, two, three, walk!" Allie commanded, sounding confident and professional.

"Don't forget to smile," Charlie whispered.

Hand in hand with her besties, Skye pulled back her toned shoulders and shook her head, rearranging her platinum wavelets so they cascaded down her back. As they made their way toward the brightness of the stage lights, she knew she couldn't possibly forget to smile—not with Charlie and Allie by her side.

For once, Shira had spoken the truth. America was waiting.

Where stories bloom.

poppy